Three Finger Exercises

A Short Story Collection

Also by Andrea Gilbey

Bottletops for Battleships: Sylvie's War

A Horse Of Course!

A Horse, Of Course! Coloring Book

A Horse, Of Course! Activity Book

You're a Big Sister!

You're a Big Brother!

Yours Ever, Notch
(a Family History in Postcards)

Three Finger Exercises

A Short Story Collection

Andrea Gilbey

Per Bastet

Three Finger Exercises

Copyright © 2018 Andrea Gilbey

Published by Per Bastet Publications LLC, P.O. Box 3023 Corydon, IN 47112

Cover photo by Andrea Gilbey

Cover design by Andrea Gilbey and T. Lee Harris

ISBN 978-1-942166-38-2

Three Finger Exercises

A Short Story Collection

Contents

Foreword

The stories in this collection were all written as writing exercises, exploring the craft, and were inspired by various prompts, both intentional and accidental.

The title describes my typing style.

I have included notes explaining the inspiration behind each story, but for those readers who prefer not to read notes until after they have completed a story, if at all, (and I include myself in that category) I have assembled them into an appendix at the back of the book.

Andrea Gilbey

The Fool On The Hill

In the time before the Great Kings, when the land was ruled by many men, there lived a king named Sigbert.

He was neither a good king nor a bad king, in the way that most people are neither wholly good nor wholly bad, but he had one besetting weakness: bronze.

He coveted, hoarded, and when unable to obtain it by honest means, stole bronze.

Chariots, thrones, bucklers, chargers, knives, pins, brooches, rings. . . . Even the decorative nails that studded the underside of his hall roof were bronze, although discoloured and stained by the smoke from the fire.

His wife, Aethelflaed, prized a disc of bronze, as wide across as the head of an ox and burnished to a shine, allowing her to admire her own beauty. For indeed Sigbert's wife was a beauty, the most beautiful woman in the kingdom, and, it was believed, all the neighbouring kingdoms.

In Sigbert's eyes, however, she was deeply flawed, as she had not presented him with an heir, and was now beyond the years of childbearing. Sigbert had sired sons and daughters by other women, as was the custom of his tribe, but none of them could inherit the kingdom or his treasure hoard when his time came to be laid in the earth.

Once his wife was past her fertile years, he ceased to bear any love for her. He ignored her and left her with only the company of her childhood nurse, an ancient woman with little hearing and fewer wits. The nurse and her own distaff and loom were the sad queen's only consolation.

1

Three Finger Exercises

By the laws of the land, a man could only cast off his wife and seek a new one if she had committed murder or adultery, or was bought by a man of equal rank for a price agreed between the two men of no less than three times her bride-price.

Sigbert knew no man of equal rank. His own laws imprisoned them both in a union as cold as bronze in shadow.

**

Aethelflaed's beauty was talked of far and wide and had come to the attention of a king named Wulfric, in a land some twenty days' march away across the river.

Wulfric was a rich widower, with three sons to inherit his own kingdom and wealth, and five daughters, all of an age to be wed. For four of his daughters, he sought marriages with neighbouring kings and their heirs, so that in time their lands could be combined into one great kingdom, stretching as far as the wide river. If he could marry his last and youngest daughter to a king across the river, then between them, the two rulers and their heirs could control all the trade that sailed the water, and tax any shipments that passed by their boundaries. If he could also find a beautiful wife to bear him company in his old age, he could die a happy man.

Sigbert's greed for bronze was known along all the trade routes of the land. Bronze traders from far distant kingdoms would refuse to sell in any of the lands along their journey, as they knew that the best prices could be had in Sigbert's domain, and only on their return journey would they part with the inferior goods rejected by the hoarder king.

**

Wulfric and his steward loaded all the bronze that their treasure-house could yield into thirty carts, bade his daughter and her servant pack chests for a journey, and with twenty of his chief warriors as guard, set out for Sigbert's land.

**

After many days' travel, they arrived at the wide river. The crossing was perilous and the boatmen unwilling to take on such a rich cargo without an equally rich fee. The carts and their precious load were tossed by the tides, and three chests of bronze goods were lost to the waves.

Wulfric's daughter was a delicate child. By the time the long procession reached Sigbert's border, she was sick with a high fever from the cold and wind and the jolting of her chariot over rough roads, so that it was all that her servant could do to encourage her to dress in her finest gown, and allow her hair to be braided with jewels fit for a queen.

Wulfric and his daughter were treated as honoured guests and feted in Sigbert's hall over three days and nights, as custom demanded, before Sigbert asked of them the purpose of their journey.

King Wulfric said, "I and my heirs rule five lands, between my kingdom and the far bank of the river. I have one daughter remaining unmarried, my youngest, Friedeswude. If you would take her as your bride, our heirs would unite the two sides of the water in one kingdom, and the river trade would be ours to control."

"But how may I marry your daughter when I am already wed to the Lady Aethelflaed?" replied King Sigbert, with never a glance at either lady.

"By the law of your land, you may be released from the bond of marriage if a man of equal rank offers more than thrice the bride-price of your wife. I, Wulfric, offer thirty carts of bronze and the hand of the Lady Friedeswude in return for the freedom of the Lady Aethelflaed to be my bride."

"What is your daughter's bride-price?"

"I ask none."

Sigbert and his advisers retired to consider the rival king's offer.

**

Three Finger Exercises

Soon the thirty carts of bronze were unloaded into Sigbert's storehouse and filled once more: this time with the Lady Aethelflaed's posessions. Sigbert was generous in allowing her to take all except her bronze mirror. The old crone, her nurse, was to remain to serve the Lady Friedeswude, now Sigbert's new queen.

The young queen was sickly, weakened by her journey, and although she conceived many times, and gave birth to several children, none of them survived infancy.

Sigbert was angry and disgusted with his queen, and spent more and more time with his hoard of bronze. He regretted having given away the beautiful Lady Aethelflaed so easily, and had his best workmen fashion a bronze sculpture of her, which he sat on a throne beside him when he dined in hall, as his sickly new wife was no ornament to his court.

The Lady Frideswude was made to keep to her quarters with the old nurse, and she became more and more unwell.

Aethelflaed, meanwhile, lived a life of leisure and luxury as Wulfric's wife, but she was unhappy. Used to being ignored and allowed to spend her hours as she pleased, it was her duty now to dress in her finest gowns, braid her hair with jewels, and preside over the high table beside her husband. Every evening was a feast, when the queen was expected to welcome and entertain visiting nobles and their wives, and supervise the provision of meats and ales for their guests. She wished that she were back at Sigbert's court, left alone to spin, weave and dream.

Time passed, as time will, and both ladies left their mortal being.

Frideswude, worn from illness and childbearing and lonely of heart, died before her time, in pain and sorrow.

Aethelflaed, having grown accustomed to her new life,

lived to a good age, and died peacefully in her sleep with her husband at her side.

Wulfric, with his chief warriors, mourned his daughter, then his wife in her turn, each for forty days and nights, in the traditional way of his tribe, and erected a stone monument to them both.

Sigbert cleared Frideswude's chambers of all but the bronze mirror and melted down the bronze statue of Aethelflaed.

***

Sigbert ruled his tribe fairly for the rest of his days, relying more and more on his steward to oversee everything except his hoard of bronze.

Daily, once his lordly business in the hall was done, he would retreat to his storehouse and remain there until it was time to eat.

His hoard increased as neighbouring chiefs vied to please him with rich gifts, in hope that the old king would name one of them his heir to avoid a war over the land when he died, but Sigbert refused to consider what would happen to his lands and people after his death. His only concern was his hoard.

In his eighty-fifth year, Sigbert was found dead, seated among his treasures, as cold as any of the metal around him in the damp, dark storehouse.

His barrow had been prepared many years before his death, as was the custom, and with proper ceremony he was interred with all his hoarded bronze, the mirror laid over his chest like a warrior's shield. His chiefs stood guard for forty days and nights, both to mourn their king and to protect the valuable mound from robbers.

***

Lying cold and still in the dark chamber, surrounded by his life's obsession, Sigbert suddenly awoke from his death sleep and sat upright.

Three Finger Exercises

There was a light in the far corner, a golden glow that pulsed and seemed to sing. The bronze mirror floated above his seated form and shone a beam toward him, blinding him.

He heard a voice like none he had ever heard before.

"Sigbert, I am come to teach you your life's lesson," the voice said, in a high, metallic tone.

"Who are you?" asked Sigbert. "Am I dead or do I live?"

"I am the earth, I am the air and the water, I am the giver of life, I am Woman," the voice replied. "You live, but only for as long as you can survive on what you spent your life to gain: bronze. You may not leave this chamber. You will live a second life: cold, shunned and ignored, as were your wives."

"A man cannot live on metal!" the king exclaimed.

"You learn well," the voice praised him. "It is a pity you could not learn this lesson in life."

The light dimmed and Sigbert was once more in darkness.

He crawled around the floor of the chamber. He knew that somewhere amongst the hoard of possessions around him was a bronze vessel filled with dried fruits: a grave gift for the gods.

His scrabbling hands slid over platters, weapons, ornaments and buckles until they found a smooth round urn. Dipping his fingers in, he pulled out some dried apples and berries and ate them hungrily. Another handful, then he stopped suddenly.

Which was the better course? To gorge and feast now, and then starve, or to ration the food, a handful or two a day, and then starve?

Either way he faced a slow and painful death.

And he was cold. He pulled the bronze mirror over himself, and dragged some of the bigger vessels around him to make a shelter, but still the cold seeped into him.

His first death had been the quiet death of an old man. This was different: To starve and freeze slowly, far from any human contact, unloved, unseen.

Andrea Gilbey

He fumbled frantically in the blackness for a large bronze axe. Desperately, he hacked at the earth above him, fighting to find a way out. His despair gave him the energy of a young warrior and his blade cut through the earth faster and faster, until a faint gleam of light showed above him.

He scrambled onto his hoarded wealth, paying no regard to it now except as a means of escape.

His hand broke the surface, then an arm. He pulled himself up until his entire upper body was free. With a gigantic effort, he escaped from his tomb. He fell to his knees, and as the warmth of the air wrapped itself around him, he felt his body grow larger and stronger. In ecstasy, arched himself towards the morning sun.

He had heard tell of the ancient race of giants; this was how they had their being, resurrected from the dark earth! His limbs stretched and grew as the warmth flooded his body until he was many times the size of a mortal man.

In an instant the burgeoning heat from the rising sun brought about a change in Sigbert: he felt a sudden chill. As the first rays of the dawn hit his body, the blood in his veins turned cold. His bones and sinews stiffened, his flesh turned hard, and his skin bloomed with a dull sheen. His brain ceased to think at all as the metal reached his very core. He had become solid bronze.

***

His giant bronze form can still be seen today, his back arched, trying to push himself out of the cold earth towards the warm sun, though time has worn it to a less than human figure. Most people call him "the Bronze Giant", but those descended from the ancient families, with old legends and stories running through their blood, call him "The Fool On The Hill."

Three Finger Exercises

Andrea Gilbey

Sylvie and the Puh

When I was really little, before I was big enough to go to school and before my sister was born, I had to go everywhere with my mum.

Daddy went to work, so he didn't have to come with us, but I went everywhere with Mummy. To the grocer's, the chemist, the library, and most boring of all, the post office.

The post office took forever, and it always seemed to be full of old ladies who all had something to say about how tall I was, how quickly I was growing up, who I looked most like, and when I was going to school. Boring.

Every day, we went somewhere, but we set aside one day a week that was our special day: Friday.

We still had to do all the shopping and the dull things, but once that was done, we would walk down into the town and have a treat.

The walk itself was a lot of fun: we went past all my favourite places on the way down the hill, and because it was treat day, we took our time and enjoyed the sights. We played a game every week: I had to try to notice three things that were funny, interesting, pretty, or unusual, then keep them to myself and remember them so I could tell Mummy about them when we came home again.

The first special place we passed was the old cottage opposite the church. Mummy said it was built before even her grandma was born, and it had an old-fashioned thatched roof and the prettiest garden I ever saw. In summer, it was full of flowers in reds, pinks, yellows and blues, and in winter the hedges were full of berries. The lady who lived there had a big fluffy ginger cat who used to sit in the window, and sometimes the lady would be sitting in the window with it and would wave to me.

The next fun thing was a place called the Green Dragon. I knew Grandma didn't like the Green Dragon; she always sniffed when Daddy said he'd been there; and Mummy said it wasn't a place for little girls, but I always liked the smell that came out of the door and, if we were really lucky on our Thursday walk, we would sometimes see big wooden barrels being rolled off a lorry and down into the cellar through a wooden trapdoor. If the trapdoor was closed I liked to tiptoe across it, pretending that a troll lived underneath, and that if I made too much noise it would jump out and catch me.

Best of all about the Green Dragon was the old bicycle that hung on the wall just inside the huge doorway that led to the yard at the back of the building. Daddy said it was called a penny farthing because it had a big wheel at the front, like a penny, and a tiny wheel at the back, like a farthing. It looked difficult to ride, maybe that was why it was just hanging on the wall.

Around the corner was the next exciting thing, and as we walked towards the humpty bridge I always asked Mummy anxiously, "You did remember, didn't you?" She always did.

Beside the humpty bridge a little grassy path led down to the river. I had to hold Mummy's hand to make sure I didn't fall in the river, but she always remembered to bring a crust of stale bread or the last dry bit of sponge cake for the ducks, and sometimes one of them would come up and take the food right out of my hand. I didn't like it so much when the geese came to see us, as they would sometimes get angry and hiss at us.

Andrea Gilbey

As we came towards the centre of town we passed the hairdresser's where Mummy had her hair set every two weeks, and if Mrs Sapsford wasn't busy doing someone's hair, we would pop in and say hello. The shop always had a lovely smell of creams and lotions, and it was cosy from the heat of the big hair-dryers where ladies sat, reading their magazines, with their heads under the hoods. In the winter, we could warm up a little and rest on the settee if no-one was waiting there for a hairdo.

Mrs Sapsford wore a pretty pink checked overall with a big pocket on the front, and sometimes she would wink at me and pull a wrapped boiled sweet out of the pocket, slipping it into my hand as though it was a secret. Mummy knew about the boiled sweets really, but she always pretended not to see, so it was a little joke between me and Mrs Sapsford.

There was just one more stop to make before we reached the main treat of the day — the toy shop. We didn't go straight in: first, we looked at all the toys in the window, big toys that were only for Christmas and birthdays. Dolls houses, bicycles, train sets and, my favourite, a toy dog on wheels. Grandma had one at her house that used to belong to my uncle, and I loved it very much, but I wished I had a real dog to play with. Mummy always said that when I was a little older we could have a dog and I could choose its name. I had already chosen his name: he would be called Scamp.

When we had examined all the toys in the window, we would go into the shop and I could choose a fourpenny toy. Sometimes it was a tiny rubber doll, sometimes a ball, and sometimes another piece for the dolls' tea set that I was collecting.

And then, at last! The end of our journey: the café.

It was my favourite place in town. It was always so warm and cosy in there: red checked cloths on all the tables, with little jam jars of flowers in the summer and berries in the winter, and the wonderful smell of cake and coffee.

Mummy always ordered a cup of coffee and a piece of Victoria sponge, and I was allowed to choose a different biscuit each week to eat with my glass of ice cold milk.

It was one of the biscuits from the café that started me learning my alphabet.

**

I sat sipping my milk and swinging my legs as I craned my neck to look around the room at all the ladies drinking tea and coffee and chatting, trying to see which cakes and biscuits they had chosen.

I picked up my own biscuit and looked closely at it. It had marks on the top that I knew were letters, but I was only just three and hadn't started learning my A B C yet.

"What does this say, Mummy?" I asked, holding my biscuit out to show her.

"The letters are Nuh, Ii, Cuh, Eh," she spelled out, "and word is 'nice', but in this case, you say it 'neece', because it's the name of a place called Nice in France."

I traced the shape of the letters on the tablecloth with my finger, repeating their sounds carefully.

"Nuh, Ii, Cuh, Eh... nice!"

"Clever girl," smiled Mummy.

She reached into her handbag, pulled out a pencil and wrote some letters on her paper napkin.

"Now try these," she turned the napkin to face me and pointed to the letters.

"Aa, Buh, Cuh, Duh. . . ."

I looked at the shapes on the tissue: I recognised the third one, it was one of the shapes on the top of the biscuit.

I repeated the sounds over and over as Mummy pointed to each letter in turn.

She took back the napkin, turned it over, and wrote a letter on the other side.

Andrea Gilbey

"Which is that, Sylvie?"

I thought hard, remembering the order of the four shapes.

"Duh!" I said, confidently, then suddenly something went "click" in my brain. "Duh for Daddy!" I shouted.

Some of the other ladies in the café turned around and smiled at me.

"Clever girl, Sylvie! Well done!" said Mummy, "But remember not to shout at the table. Now, what is this letter?"

She drew a curved shape on the paper and I thought of the curved back of the cat at the thatched cottage.

"Cuh for cat!" I laughed. This was fun!

***

And that was how I started to learn the alphabet. Every Friday morning I learned a few more letters at the café until I could say the whole alphabet right through and recognise all the letters on their own without getting any wrong.

***

One Friday morning I remember especially, because something funny happened.

It was just after Christmas: I remember because I was wearing my red Christmas pixie hood and Mummy had on a new hat with a big band of fur that came down right over her ears.

We had enjoyed our walk down to town, I had a blackcurrant boiled sweet tucked in my pocket for later, and I had chosen a crumbly Viennese whirl with cream and jam in the middle to go with my glass of milk.

I had my three special things to tell Mummy about, so I was ready when she asked me, as we turned into our road, "So, what did you notice today, Sylvie?"

I counted the things off on my fingers as I recited them.

"There was a lady in the café wearing a hat with a little robin on the side of it, I thought that was really pretty."

"Oh yes," Mummy said, as she squeezed my hand, "it looked lovely, didn't it! Maybe her hat was a Christmas present, too, just like ours. What else?"

"Mrs Sapsford's hair was a different colour today! Isn't that odd? I didn't know people's hair could change colour!"

Mummy had a sudden fit of coughing, so we stood still until she felt better.

"Sometime's people's hair changes colour as they get older." She smiled. "My hair was fair like yours when I was your age, but it got darker as I grew older; I expect yours will, too."

Mrs Sapsford's hair had got lighter, not darker, but I guessed it was One Of Those Things that grown-ups won't tell you about, so I moved on to my third interesting thing.

"Outside the Green Dragon there was a Puh in the road!"

Mummy stopped dead and stared at me.

"What? Oh! Why didn't you say at the time?"

She rummaged frantically in her bag.

"At least it's not mine, but we'd better go back and get it, someone will be looking for it."

She turned on her heel and half-ran half-walked back the way we came, dragging me with her. I was confused: why would anyone be looking for a Puh?

As we trotted towards the Green Dragon Mummy was searching the ground all around us.

"Where did you see it?" she asked me urgently.

"There."

I pointed to the large white letter P that had been painted on the road outside the building.

"Where? I can't see it?"

"There: a big Puh in the road. Puh for pig."

Mummy dropped my hand, looked at the road, looked back at me, and covered her face with her hands.

I could feel my eyes going all blurry and my lip trembling.

Andrea Gilbey

I'd made Mummy cry! What was so awful about there being a P in the road? What did it mean?

Mummy took her hands away from her face and I could see it was bright red. My eyes brimmed over with tears.

Suddenly she burst out laughing and laughed and laughed until she could hardly breathe. I didn't know whether to be relieved or even more worried, and the tears kept coming.

Finally she stopped laughing and crouched beside me, grabbing me in a big hug.

"Oh, Sylvie," she croaked, wiping her eyes. "I thought you said you saw a *purse* in the road!" She pushed her hat up away from her ears and shook her head.

"I can't hear properly through all this fur. I'm sorry, darling, I didn't mean to scare you, I really thought you said "purse". I think we need to move you on to the next stage of learning the alphabet and teach you the proper names for the letters!"

She took my hand and chanted as we skipped back towards home, "Ayy, Bee, Cee, Dee. . . ."

Three Finger Exercises

Andrea Gilbey

The Ship's Carpenter

"Jake? Jake! Where are you?"

Christ, you hear of this, but you don't ever think it will happen to your kid, you think you've got them under your eye, that you've told them about not wandering off and they get it, but when it happens. . . .

I went cold all over when I realised I couldn't see him. We were in a strange place, in a strange town, and he'd just vanished from under my nose.

Calm down, I told myself. He's small, he could just be behind one of the displays and looking at a video or something and not listening. If you sound panicked, he'll panic. Be calm, be quiet, but move fast.

I started pacing the gallery, methodically checking over and behind each of the free-standing displays, calling his name in what I hoped was a happy, positive, Daddy's-not-at-all-scared voice. Louise will kill me, was all I could think. How could I go home and tell her I'd lost our son?

The stairs — there were three levels to the exhibition spaces at each end of the main gallery, maybe he had slipped back down the stairs to look at something again; the video of the ship's carpenter, maybe, he'd liked that, especially the bit about the dog.

The uniformed attendant at the top of the stairs shook her head. No, no small children had passed her. She pursed her lips slightly as she replied and a white-hot anger shot through me as, in my panicked state, I thought I sensed her disapproval of my fecklessness in losing my child among strangers. I wanted to yell at her, "I am a responsible father! He just . . . vanished!"

I hurried over to the lift, doing that heels down first scuttle that you do when you're trying to hurry but not look flustered. Surely, he hadn't got in the lift? He was barely tall enough to press the buttons.

I hadn't even considered that he may have gone out into the main gallery. The doors at each end on this floor were air-locked to protect the five-hundred-year-old ship from as much contamination and drying as possible. Visitors had to wait in the lobby between the doors for a red light to come on, then press the release button to open the innermost doors. He was only just four: he wouldn't be able to work that out.

I'd forgotten that this is the digital age. He was playing games on my tablet at two: a simple door release would be child's play, literally.

The attendant by the gallery entrance noticed my badly hidden panic.

"Is that your little lad in there?" he asked, nodding at the double glass doors.

Jake! He was running up and down the long narrow gallery, occasionally looking behind him and laughing, then dodging and running back the other way.

It was a quiet morning: hardly anyone around, and too early for school parties, so my son had the whole gallery to himself to play whatever game he was playing.

I reached out to press the button for the door, but the guard stopped me, gently.

"Leave him a while, he's enjoying himself and he'll come to no harm there. I've been keeping an eye on him for a few minutes and. . . ."

The man stopped, awkwardly, and glanced at me.

"What's the matter? Has he been touching something he shouldn't?"

"No, no, not at all. He can't, in the gallery, anyway. Everything that's open is meant to be touched and the rest is safe behind glass. No, it's just . . . well, I've seen this before, not just with kids, although the very little kids are more accepting of this kind of thing."

I looked at him encouragingly, but blankly. What on earth was he on about?

The man looked around him. Obviously, what he was about to say was not official museum policy, or something.

"This ship . . . technically it's a grave site. I know it's been raised and cleaned and preserved and all that, but all those men lived and died on there. I'm no psychic or seer, and I would've laughed at what I'm about to tell you before I came to work here, but I've seen the way people act, and there is something, or someone, here that some people can sense."

I looked back through the glass doors at my happy child. He was still running up and down, as though chasing or being chased by someone, occasionally stooping and clapping his hands, as though encouraging an animal to come to him.

He certainly didn't look like the subject of a haunting, if that's what the guard was trying to say.

The looped sound effects in the gallery sounded faintly through the doors. There's a recording of a dog barking, I thought: Jake's just pretending there's a real animal there, playing that the dog that belonged to the ship's carpenter is running up to him.

"He's just messing about," I reassured the attendant. "He's obsessed with the idea of a dog on board the ship. He spent ages looking at the poor mutt's skeleton downstairs."

Jake stopped running and stood still, miming stroking an animal. He was an imaginative little boy at the best of times, but his actions looked completely realistic. I briefly considered finding an acting class for him.

He abruptly looked up and stepped back a pace from the invisible pet, his eyes focussed at adult head height, listening intently, then nodded and reached out to take something from the air. He knelt and held his hand out flat to the unseen pooch, just as I had shown him when I took him to the petting area at our local farm to feed the baby goats.

I looked at my companion and he held my gaze, steadily, calmly, but with a world of understanding in his eyes.

"It happens a lot," he said gently, "people spend hours in the ship galleries, just gazing at the hull and . . . communing with the spirits, I suppose you could say, but that sounds fanciful. I've watched those projected tableaux over and over; I know every detail of what those actors do in each scene, but now and then someone will come over to talk and describe seeing something that isn't in the script. They don't all realise what they're seeing, of course. And some don't see, they just feel.

"I've had people tell me they can feel the old sailors watching them and wondering what all these people are doing, staring at the wreck of their old ship and picking over their ordinary possessions like they're treasures.

"But all of them say they feel warmth, and a sense of purpose; there's no feeling of fear or tragedy, which is odd, considering that she went down with the loss of almost all hands."

As I listened to the attendant, my eyes drifted back to Jake, who was standing still, his left hand absently stroking his invisible canine friend, his face turned up to some other presence that was hidden from my eyes, occasionally speaking, then listening.

I wanted to walk through there and hear what he was saying, but I knew that, as soon as he heard the doors open, his concentration would be broken. Better to watch and wait.

The recorded tableaux started up again, and ghostly seamen went about their business on various parts of the preserved wreck, accompanied by sound effects that faintly penetrated the end gallery where I stood.

Jake's gaze lowered and his head turned as he looked back and forth from his invisible companion, who seemed to be crouching beside him now, to the ship and the projected scenes, nodding, speaking, listening and occasionally laughing.

The recorded action came to an end and Jake stepped back from the glass railing, patted the dog that by now I could almost see, then held out his small hand in an oddly formal farewell handshake. He gazed towards the doors at the other end of the gallery for a long moment, then waved and turned his attention back to the ship.

Shaken, I met the kind eyes of my companion again. He smiled sympathetically, patted my shoulder, then reached out for the button to operate the door.

"Ready? Remember, he's seen nothing that was surprising to him. Let him tell you if and when he wants to."

I nodded and passed through the door, using the few seconds in the air lock to compose my face into a relaxed smile.

"Hey, big man, there you are." He turned and grinned at me. I hated to spoil his fun, but I had to let him know that the way he'd behaved in leaving the gallery was out of order.

"When we get back to the car you and I need a little talk about you wandering off, don't we?" I said gently, crouching down beside him.

He nodded, crestfallen.

"I'm sorry, Daddy, I forgot, but I didn't go outside, you could see me through the door, and I was with that man. . . ," he tailed off, realising that he'd also broken the "stranger danger" rule, tears gleaming on his flushed cheeks.

I hugged him tight.

"All right, then, lesson learned and apology accepted: you won't do it again, will you?"

He shook his head dumbly.

"So, what did the man say?" I asked airily.

"Well, he thought I might be scared of his dog, so he came to see if I was OK and I told him I like dogs. He said the dog's name is Hatch. It's a funny name, isn't it, but he said that's what the holes in the decks are called that you open to climb down the ladders to the next deck. He told me lots of new words about ships; the house bit on the top is called the castle, the ropes that hold the sails up are called sheets, and he said there's a thing called a dead eye that the ropes go 'round. That's creepy, isn't it!" he ended with relish.

The only thing that was creeping was my spine. Jake could read a bit: "the cat sat on the mat" kind of reading: but no way could he have learned those words by reading the displays in the exhibition, and I hadn't read them aloud to him unless he asked me to. I could remember my dad solemnly reading every notice to me as a kid, going around museums, and recalled how boring it was when there were buttons to be pressed and things to touch elsewhere.

"He sounds like he knows a lot about ships," I commented, trying to draw my little son into further revelations.

"He works here," he replied.

"Oh, he's one of the guides who dress up and explain how people lived in the olden days?" I suggested. Jake shook his head impatiently.

"No, he works *there*." He pointed towards one of the open sections of the ship. "He's the carpenter, he mends things."

The tableaux started up again and we watched as an actor used a plane on a piece of wood, his dog running around his feet.

"Is that him, your friend the carpenter?" I asked, pointing in my turn.

"No, *he's* not a real carpenter, he's just pretending. My friend said that man doesn't know one end of a plane from another," he laughed at the joke and I joined in, laughing as much at his glee as at the joke.

I tried another question, holding myself back, not wanting to scare my boy, but wanting to share whatever had happened and feeling mildly envious that I was somehow outside this brief relationship that had developed between my son and his new friend.

"So where does he live, then?" I asked casually, studying the information board by the railing.

"Here, on the ship, of course."

"But the ship's not a whole ship any more, is it?" I probed gently.

I could see that Jake was trying not to roll his eyes in despair at his dim-witted father and bit back a smile.

"He doesn't live on it *now*, he lives on it *then*."

I nodded silently, awed at the child's imagination that could encompass such an idea with complete acceptance.

"So, any plans to be a sailor? Or maybe a carpenter?" I took my son's hand and gently swung his arm as we walked towards the exit.

He shook his head firmly.

"No, I want to make computer games when I grow up," he paused and looked up at me. "Daddy, can I ask you a question?"

Here it comes, I thought.

"Of course, champ, fire away."

"Can we get a dog? And can we call him Hatch?"

I laughed, relieved. People were filling the gallery now, waiting for the next projector show to start, murmuring quietly in the subdued light.

"We'll talk to your mum about that when we get home, shall we? Now, let's go and find something to eat. I don't know about you, but I'm starving!"

He skipped beside me as we approached the air-locked doors at the far end of the gallery. As the doors hissed open he turned back and waved. Almost as a reflex I turned too and looked over my shoulder, and for just a moment I thought I saw a white sleeve flutter and a hand wave, and the faint sound of a dog barking.

Andrea Gilbey

Harvest Homecoming

Joe mooched around the edge of the field, watching the bustle of activity. Stallholders yelled, advertising their wares, fairground rides blared tinny music, vying with the Beatles and Stones tunes coming from the lemonade stand, and the place thronged with teenage girls in calico and gingham dresses in the fashions of the late eighteen hundreds, twirling, flirting, putting on rural "farm girl" accents and talking about "Ma" and "Pa". Joe listened to their chatter and grinned to himself. If they'd listened to as many old timers' farm stories as he'd had to sit through from his great grandma they'd be back in their Capri pants and ponytails like a shot. It wasn't all sitting on the porch knitting as the sun went down over fields of corn, he could tell them!

Joe could never decide whether he liked Harvest Homecoming or not. He liked the parade, and his favourite part was the week before, when all the older men would come to him to help them tinker up the old jalopies they were going to drive in it, but he wasn't so fond of the fair; it was all a bit loud and brash.

His narrow chest swelled wider with pride as he thought of the parade. He was gaining a good reputation as a mechanic now, and he had overheard one or two of the men telling their friends, "Y'know she wouldn't be running at all if it weren't for young Joe Matthews."

Of course, tinkering with all the old cars took his time away from his precious Camaro, but the restoration was nearly finished now, just the seats to be re-upholstered; and the goodwill of the older men of the town would do him well if he set up his own repairs garage when he finished school.

Wandering around, seeing his classmates playing, teasing, fighting, he sighed to himself. He was a quiet boy who only really opened up around his few closest friends, who, unluckily for them, had been roped in by mothers and older sisters to help in the various booths, so today he was strolling alone, smiling, trying to look as though being on his own at Harvest Homecoming was making him the happiest person alive.

He bought a corn dog from one of the booths and ambled down towards the bottom of the field, gazing around at the activity. Rounding the corner of the old derelict barn, he found himself face to face with a petite girl in pioneer costume, her auburn hair hanging in braids over her shoulders. Hastily, quietly, he stepped backwards, not wanting to be forced to make conversation, but it was too late, she had seen him and she smiled, a shy smile, showing small teeth in a mouth that tilted slightly upwards at one side.

He smiled back and wished her a good afternoon.

"Are you enjoying the fair?" he ventured, after a short uncomfortable silence.

"Oh yes, I come every year, I wouldn't miss Harvest Homecoming for the world!"

Her eyes shone, and there was that quirky smile again. Something about her seemed familiar, and very likeable.

"Do you go to school around here?"

"I used to," she replied, "I left two years ago. I was never going to be smart enough to get a teacher's certificate, and Ma needed some help on the farm. My littlest sister is just four, and she's quite a handful."

"You can't be more than sixteen," he exclaimed. "How come your folks let you leave school so young?"

"I'm seventeen, eighteen next March." She drew herself up to her full five feet and looked at him haughtily.

"Okay! Sorry!"

"Okay?" she asked, tilting her head on one side so her face was half shaded by her sprigged cotton sunbonnet.

"I . . . I mean of course you are . . . I mean . . . yes ma'am." He shuffled his feet and looked down at his shiny cockroach killers, then glanced up to check her mood and found her looking him over from head to toe with a quizzical expression, from his tight shoes and drainpipe jeans up to his striped t shirt and bomber jacket.

"I . . . er, I don't really like dressing up," he muttered, excusing his anachronistic outfit.

The girl burst out laughing, her eyes crinkled up and she laughed full and loud, a proper guffaw, not an affected titter like the cheerleader types at school.

"I'd never have guessed." She smiled. "You look just fine, a little different, but fine."

He blushed, and the toes of his shoes came in for some more intense scrutiny.

"Do you want to maybe take a walk and have a look at the tractor pull?" he asked diffidently.

"Tractor pull?" she frowned, wrinkling her nose and looked up at him, confused.

"Er, yeah, over there, look, the men are lining up to see how far they can pull Sherman's big old tractor."

"I think you have a touch of the sun, that's my uncle Bill with the plowing contest."

Joe looked back down at her, confused in his turn.

"Well, whatever you call it, shall we go look?"

"I'd rather stay here and just talk," she replied shyly.

"Wooohoooo!" a piercing yell split the air, louder even than the fairground barkers.

"Old Joey-boy's found hisself a girlfriend! I bet he's tellin' her all kinds of rivetin' stuff about engines."

Joe's face burned red and he looked at his companion with an expression of agony.

"Ignore them, it's just some jocks from my school."

"Lemme get a snap of the happy couple," the boy yelled, as his coterie of followers sniggered.

"Say cheese!" The boy pointed a Polaroid camera at the embarrassed pair and snapped away.

Joe's companion took a step forward, and he put a hand on her arm for a second, then, scared at his own temerity, removed it again.

"I think some people 'round here need a lesson in manners," the girl stormed, hands on hips, eyes flashing.

"Wooooo!" jeered the boys again, but they backed down and strolled away. No fun in baiting a girl.

"I'm sorry." Joe looked at his feet.

"It's . . . okay . . . Joey, or do you prefer Joe?"

"Joe," he replied. "No-one calls me Joey except those . . . idiots."

"And I'm Grace." The girl held out a small slim hand for him to shake.

"My mom's name's Grace; that's a good name," grinned Joe, gently pumping her hand.

They smiled at each other for a long minute, then Grace coughed slightly and glanced down at their joined hands. Joe let go as though he had been holding a hot potato.

"So . . . er . . . Grace, can I . . . may I . . . um . . . I'dreallyliketoseeyouagain."

Grace smiled.

"I'd like that, too. Maybe after church on Sunday?"

"I could come pick you up after service. Where do you go?"

"Up there, the big white church on the hill. Service finishes at midday. Oh, and there's a hitching post around the side."

Joe felt a chill as though he had stepped in cold water. He looked up towards the empty hill. There was no church there; he knew there had been; his great grandma had talked about it, said it burnt down in the late 1880s.

"Hitching p. . . ?" he turned to look at Grace but the girl had vanished. He scanned the crowd, but there were so many girls in frilled bonnets and sprigged dresses, and she was so tiny. . . .

"Are you all right son? Joe? Earth calling Joseph?"

"Mom! Sorry, I was miles away."

"You look sick, boy, what's the matter?"

"I guess I've been standing in the sun too long. I think I'll go get myself a cold root beer."

"Here's a dollar, treat yourself to some candy and a hotdog, too."

"Thanks Mom." He kissed her on the cheek and loped away to the side of the field where the food stalls were congregated, flipping the dollar bill between his fingers with no idea of what he was doing, his great-grandma's voice echoing in his head.

It was a Harvest Homecoming some thirteen years earlier, and five-year-old Joe was standing beside his great-grandma's wheelchair, shifting impatiently from one foot to the other and holding a parasol over the old lady's head as she gossiped and reminisced about the families and buildings of the town in days long gone, the boy only half listening to her stories.

"Of course there used to be a church up on that hill, big white church, but it burnt down one Sunday after service. My grandma was just a little girl of four, but she remembered it well, the tragedy. The superintendent was burning leaves at the side of the church and left the fire to go for his mid-day dinner. A wind came up and the church caught. It was gone in minutes, all timber framed, you see. Poor Grace. . . ."

Grace... the name rang in his head.

A shoulder jostled into him. The boy with the Polaroid — what was his name, Steve? Dave?

Three Finger Exercises

"Lost your sweetie, then? She not into greasy engineers? Here's a memento of your little romance." He tucked a small square of card into Joe's top pocket, patted it, and swaggered off, surrounded by giggling girls.

Joe bought a root beer and a hot dog and sat down on a barrel in the shade behind one of the booths. He methodically ate the hotdog, tasting nothing, and washed it down with half the root beer before taking the photo out of his pocket. There she was, half laughing, half angry as the stranger snapped her picture. Did she even understand what he was doing, if she was. . . ?

But she couldn't be . . . could she?

⁂

"I brought you out an ice tea, Mom. Mind if I sit with you a while?"

"Oh, thank you Joe, sit yourself down. You look tired. You've had a long week working on all those cars."

He nodded and sipped at his tea.

"Mom, do you remember Great-grandma talking about a church up on the hill overlooking the fairground? And a fire? Something from her grandma's time?"

"Oh, goodness, yes, that was a very sad story. It was her grandma's older sister who died in the fire. The superintendent left a bonfire blazing and the church went up in flames. Poor Grace was in the church: apparently, she'd arranged to meet a boy after service and he was late, so she went back in the church to sit down and fell asleep. I remember my grandma saying they always prayed that she knew nothing about what happened to her, that the fire took hold so fast, maybe she never woke up. My great-great-grandma was only four at the time, so she didn't really understand how awful it was until she was older. Poor Grace. Sweet-looking girl she was, too, very petite. That's why I was called Grace, to keep her memory alive."

"Is there . . . do you have a portrait of her? Were there photos back then?"

"Oh yes, it was quite the fad to get a family portrait done when the photographer came to town. People saved for months to pay for it. Let me go look. I think it's in the trunk in the back room."

She heaved herself up from the swing seat with a groan and headed into the house. Glancing around to make sure no-one was watching, Joe took the photo out of his pocket and studied the animated little face that had seemed so familiar to him.

Hearing his mother returning, he slipped the photo away again, and sipped at his drink, trying to control shaking hands.

"Here." The modern-day Grace placed a faded cardboard folder on his lap and he slowly opened the cover. "This is the photo with my Great-great-auntie Grace in it. She's . . . there, look, second from the end. And that's your great-grandma's grandma, the little girl in the front. This was taken the Christmas before Grace died."

Joe's eyes swam and he swallowed hard. There she was. The same lop-sided smile, the same twinkle in her eyes. Grace. He cleared his throat.

"That . . . that's cool, Mom, that you still have this after all these years to remember her by. That poor boy, I feel sorry for him, too."

"What boy?" asked his mother, taking the precious photo away out of reach of wet glasses and cold drinks.

"The boy she arranged to meet. I wonder what happened, why he didn't show. He must've felt awful when he heard what happened to her."

"You know, I never thought about him, in all the times I've heard the story."

She patted Joe on the shoulder.

"You're a sweet caring boy. Some girl's going to be very lucky one day."

He bowed his head over his drink, acting shy to hide brimming tears until he got them under control. He drained his glass and stood up.

"I think I'll go out to the garage for a while, tinker on the Camaro."

"Okay, but don't be out there too late, you've had a rough week, you need to get an early night."

Joe sat in the car, but for once his pride in his work meant nothing. He might as well have been sitting in the rusted heap of junk he'd bought two years earlier.

He placed the photo on the steering wheel and looked into the eyes of the girl in the picture.

"I'm sorry, Grace."

He opened the glove box flap and felt at the side of the lining panel, easing it away from the interior until he had a slot big enough, then slipped the photo inside and pushed the panel back. He could fix it properly in the morning.

Andrea Gilbey

Sid and the Unicorn

I hated the Unicorn when it first arrived. It didn't do anything to upset me, but that was just it, it didn't do anything at all. It just sat there, all pink and white and sparkly.

I'm Sid, by the way: Sidney actually, but everyone here calls me Sid. Truth be told, I feel more like a Sidney inside: I like to listen to a bit of classical music when I've got the house to myself, you know, the finer things in life.

Oh, and I'm a dog.

**

The Small Female Human brought the Unicorn into the house: apparently, it was a gift from her godmother. I haven't met the godmother, but it seems she's also my fairy-dogmother too, whatever that means.

So the SFH dumped this Unicorn down on the sofa where I was having a nap. I sniffed it, nudged it with my nose, licked its face, which tasted awful, not like proper fur at all, but it just sat there smiling that stupid smile with its tongue out. Maybe it was a bit . . . simple?

I decided to ignore it, but the SFH wasn't having that. The Unicorn had to be in on our fun, whatever we did. I love it when she cuddles up on the sofa with me, but now there were three of us in the cuddles, and one of us had a really fluffy mane and tail, enough to make a dog sneeze.

I would sometimes "accidentally" shoot my leg out, pretending I had an itch, and knock old Pink & Fluffy to the floor, but it would be rescued and put back beside me.

I dragged it into another room and left it there, but a few minutes later it was back. There was no escape. It even came on walks with us, although it had to be carried as its stupid little legs wouldn't hold it up.

**

When I get home from my walk I like to curl up on the sofa for a nap, which is exactly what I did yesterday afternoon. I was just settling down to sleep when I felt something on the cushion behind me. I opened one eye and peeped. Yep. The Unicorn. SFH had sat it so it was staring at me with its goofy smile and little poppy eyes. I hunched my shoulder and ignored it.

"I just want to be friends."

What? Who said that?

I lifted my head and opened my eyes. The Unicorn was grinning at me, and there was the voice again.

"I said, I just want to be friends."

"Umm . . . you can talk?" I asked it.

"Yes, and so can you, or how else are we having this conversation?"

I thought about that for a while. Of course I can talk, other dogs know exactly what I'm saying, and sometimes SFH understands me, but I can't say human words. The Unicorn's thin pink mouth didn't move when it spoke, so maybe we were communicating by thought.

"You're not . . . real, are you?" I didn't want to hurt its feelings, but it needed to be said.

"Depends what you mean by real," it replied.

It was obvious that I would have to spell it out, whether the truth hurt or not.

"I mean, you don't move, you don't eat, you don't poop, you don't breathe . . . you're not . . . real!"

The grin didn't waver for a second.

"Let me ask you something," the Unicorn said. "You're

adopted, aren't you? The SFH and her family aren't your real family. I mean, they're not dogs, so they can't be."

"Yes, I'm adopted," I said quietly, "but . . . but they love me, and I love them; I belong with them, they are my family, real or not."

"Exactly," said the Unicorn, smugly.

"Exactly what?" I didn't see its point.

"These humans are your family because they love you and you love them, right? Well the SFH, as you call her, loves me. Her godmother made me for her because she loves her god-daughter. So all that love makes me real.

"Oh, I'll never be as real as you. I can't run and play with her like you can, but I'm not just a bundle of fabric and stuffing any more, I'm real to someone. I belong.

"You're real in your way, I'm real in mine. Our SFH loves us and we love her, so can't we just be friends?"

I thought long and hard. It had a point. It couldn't chase a ball and bring it back to SFH to be thrown again, it couldn't shake itself all over her and make her laugh, but she could tuck it under her arm and take it with her to places where I wouldn't want to go. Big girl that she is now, sometimes everyone needs something small and fluffy to cuddle . . . even me. . . .

I wriggled over to the Unicorn and kissed its nose.

"Friends?" I looked at it with my head on one side.

"Friends," it smiled.

I snuffled its face and settled down to sleep again.

**

Click!

"Mum, look, isn't Sid sweet, all curled up with the Unicorn? I took a photo!" SFH called to the Bigger Female Human.

"I think he was dreaming. He was making funny little noises and waving his paws around," she said as she showed the BFH something on the little thin box she carries around with her everywhere.

Three Finger Exercises

I opened my eyes and puffed pink fur away from my nose.

The Unicorn still had that fixed smile on its face, but for just a second I thought I saw it wink.

Andrea Gilbey

A Plague On Both Your Houses.

Here we go, the usual tuneless whistle that means dinner is served. Leftovers for the less fortunate, namely, yours truly.

Looks like it's just me today, everyone else must be busy, or just not hungry, if such a state is possible.

I've been coming here for a few years now; the food changes every once in a while; it's not always the same people here, you see. Him Upstairs, he's the one that owns the place, the tenants downstairs don't usually stay very long, can't imagine why.

This pair, though, I like. I've been in the house a fair few times, and other houses round here. I've seen people making their meals, cooking at the stoves, stirring, baking, roasting, but not these two. They don't keep a scrap of fresh food in the cupboards. I've had a good look round while they were out, but it's all dry stuff, pasta and rice, which they don't ever seem to use. They don't notice when some of it goes missing, anyway.

No, these two buy all their food in, in boxes, then when they've had enough, they just open the back door and lob what's left outside for the likes of me to collect. Sometimes they throw out the boxes, too, which come in useful.

Oh, it's not charity, the chucking out, they're just lazy; too lazy to even put the scraps in a dustbin, which doesn't bother me. It makes my life easier.

Her Next Door's not best amused, though; turns her nose

up in disgust. I never get any scraps from her, nothing gets wasted in that house. Plus, she's got two cats, so I don't go near. Me and cats don't exactly see eye to eye.

So, what's on the menu today? Fish and chips, lovely! Nice big bit of fish, enough there to take some home for the missus and the little'uns.

Didn't know I was married, did you? Big family, I've got, so now and then a bit of scrounging's necessary.

Oops! Here he comes again. Better nip behind the shed; I'd rather he didn't know I was here. What's he chucked out now? Cake! Chocolate muffin, bit stale, but needs must.

I nearly got caught the other day; he left the door open as it was a warm evening, so in I popped while his back was turned. He does this off-key whistling all the time, so I knew he wouldn't hear me. He was making tea — about the only cooking that gets done in that kitchen — and he'd left the food open on the table. Chinese, it was. Well, I was just about to help myself to a nice big mouthful of sweet and sour pork, when in she walked. She was reading something to him, a letter, it looked like, so she didn't look up and I had time to slide out the door, but it was a close thing.

She was in quite a state about the letter. Seems someone had reported them to Him Upstairs for "insanitary conditions". Probably Mrs Snooty next door. Anyway, it saved my bacon that time.

I think I've got enough for today, I'll come back tomorrow and see what's on offer.

∗∗∗

So I got caught.

It had to happen some time; it happens to us all eventually, occupational hazard when you live this kind of life.

It was pizza: Hawaiian, I think, and he'd just slung the box out with a slice and a half in it. What he didn't realise was that he'd dropped a nice big piece of ham just inside the door, and then trodden on it as he went back in.

Well, I couldn't let that go to waste, could I? Trouble was, it was covered in cheese on the floor side, stuck fast to the kitchen tiles. I suppose you could say greed got the better of me, and while I was busy scraping it up, I forgot to be wary. First thing I know, there's a plastic bowl flying across the room, aimed right at my head.

"Get out of here, you filthy creature," he yells at me. Well, pots and kettles, I think to myself, but there you go.

Then she comes in and all hell breaks loose. Screaming, crying, jumping on a chair.

"Ohmygodohmygod! A RAT! It's probably got plague and fleas and everything!"

Well, I couldn't help myself; I ran under her chair and gnawed the leg a bit, then I bruxed and boggled at her for good luck, and ran out the door.

The only good thing: they don't own a broom, or I suspect I'd have been ejected faster than I can run.

Oh well, it was good while it lasted. I suppose I'll have to look elsewhere. Maybe I'll just hang around in Mrs Snooty's garden and pull faces at her cats through the window.

Live dangerously, eh?

Three Finger Exercises

Turbine Or Not Turbine

"My arms ache, don't yours?"

If Enti Bur had possessed eyes in her current mutation she would have rolled them at the lame joke. Once again, she was transmitting on her personal frequency instead of using the group signal, thus leaving Bert Inu out of the conversation. With two hundred demi-quadrants of ground between them it was unlikely to get him anywhere with her physically, if that was his idea.

She switched to the three-way frequency before replying.

"Very funny. Again. Not. Ben Turi, why do you have to fight everything?"

"What do you mean?" his sharp reply crackled on her sensor.

She sent out vision waves in his direction. Yet again, his sails were turning at half the speed of hers and Bert's.

"You even fight the wind. Just let go and allow your sails to do their work."

Enti had enjoyed her new shape from the start. She loved her two elegant long sails and her tall white stem that lifted her high above the countryside. It had taken her a while to get used to the damp greenness of this strange planet, but after . . . she thought hard; was it really three dark seasons and two light that they had been here? . . .she felt completely at home.

"If the Grand Council wants to punish me by sending me here to live inside a . . . a . . . machine, and suck up my nutrition from the dirt of this worn-out planet, I'm damned if I'll co-operate. Why should I help these pathetic humans? They'd be better served by selling this land and building their stupid little living-pods on it."

"We've been over this before," transmitted Bert. "I don't understand why you think we were sent here for punishment. You were at the same briefing as us. We were sent here to learn how this planet works and help these humans understand how to use what they have. I still can't believe that they think digging liquid out of the ground and setting fire to it is the best way to create energy."

His friends felt little buffeting puffs of air as he sent them the version of a chuckle that he had invented by repeatedly slowing his sails for a second at a time.

"We were sent to educate these beings and show them how to protect their living environment. They have a lot to learn," commented Enti sadly.

"You two seem to have different interpretations of the briefing." Ben's message flashed like lightning. "What if the Grand Council transmitted a different briefing to each of us at the same time?"

"Can't be done," replied Bert flatly, dismissing Ben's paranoia. "It's not possible to transmit separate messages on three different personal frequencies at once."

"How do you know?"

"Who set up the system for the Grand Council?" The buffeting breeze jolted against their sails again.

"And you're the genius who developed a way of sending signals to humans that they sometimes understand, we know," sneered Ben. All the signals Ben sent to the humans had either been misunderstood or not delivered, as he had yet to make any impression on their behaviour. In trying to convince them to sell the field for development, he was hoping that the Grand Council would have to send a ship to take its stranded missionaries/exiles home again.

"Oh, hold on, look: three quadrants anti from magnetic positive. We've got company." Bert's transmission was fast, but none of them needed to check their magnetic direction sensors by now. They had been static for so long that they knew every milli-quadrant of the area. Three sets of vision waves were directed to the point where a vehicle was parked at the entrance to the field and three humans in orange over-vests and white hats walked slowly towards the three towers, consulting papers on boards held in their hands.

The three beings in the towers tuned their receptors to human speech and waited.

"Number two's on a go-slow again," said one of the humans, making a note. "I don't get it. They're made the same, positioned facing the same way, programmed the same, so why is number two consistently under-performing?"

"The telemetry doesn't show any anomaly in the electronics." The female human frowned. "It doesn't make sense."

"I'm seriously considering adding another sail blade to all three of them. This early design was good for the technology we had a few years ago, but they really need replacing now."

Enti and Ben felt buffeting waves of excitement from Bert. He had been steadily transmitting the idea of three sails for greater efficiency over the whole of the last light season and it seemed that the message was getting through.

The third human spoke without looking up from his notes.

"No point in tinkering with number two. I think we should cut our losses and scrap it. It hasn't been any good for the last two and a half years."

**

The three friends emerged gratefully from their underground supply pods, each remembering the rush to dig them down into the soft sandy soil below the tower bases when they had arrived on that miserable wet darkphase so long ago.

Each slithered back up the tall stem and settled in the head of the device, replaced and re-set their communications channels and scanned the others' towers with their vision waves.

"Oh, very smart, you two." Ben's was the first signal to break the silence. "Now you've got to work half as hard again."

"Think yourself lucky you're still standing," replied Bert. "I thought you were for the scrap heap."

"I entreat the Being of Beings every darkphase for that to happen so I can go home. Back to the name I'm known by, back to my own pod, maybe even start my own colony. What d'you say, Enti? Care to come back and be my mate?"

Enti ignored the comment.

"Did you two project vision waves while we were in the supply pods? Did you see how they laid tracks to protect the crops and how they removed every last trace of metal from the field when they finished? I persuaded them to do that." Her message was full of pride and satisfaction.

"I will stay here as long as it takes to teach these humans how to treat their world. And who could want to be away from this view? I have nothing to go back home for, and maybe one day I can mutate again into one of the animals that live on this land. What about you, Bert?"

A peaceful sigh of air wafted across from the sails of the third tower.

"I'm happy here. Maybe the natural nutritional stuff is a bit hard to get used to, but we must be due a supply ship at the next Darkphase to refill the pods. There's a lot more work for me to do here before I'm finished. Did you hear the human that owns the land talking about building a dam in the river to harness the power of the water? My idea."

"The two of you have gone native. . . ."

Ben's transmission was interrupted by a crackle of static and a strange metallic sound somewhere between a whistle and a hiss.

"The Grand Council!" The exclamation bounced between the three receptors.

"Your progress has been monitored," the transmission began, with no salutation of any kind. "Enti Bur, we are satisfied with you. You have encouraged an understanding of the nature of this world in its inhabitants, and it is becoming a happier, more peaceful place because of you.

"Bert Inu, you are showing these humans how to use the natural energy of their world for the better. Maybe soon they will start to understand our communications with their minds as well as their instincts. We are satisfied with you.

"When you both reach your next mutation, you will be given a choice of being, as a sign of our regard. It has been recorded in your life journals.

"Ben Turi. You have let us down. Your thoughts have been of nothing but yourself. You have not contributed in any way to this planet's well being, or that of its inhabitants. Your tower is to be dismantled over the next few Lightphases. At the midst of the next Darkphase you must mutate. You do not have a choice of being; you will mutate as you are instructed when the time comes."

The transmission ended as abruptly as it began, leaving no sound except the swoosh of eight sails against the air.

"Well." Ben's signal was faint. "I guess this is goodbye, then. I wonder what they'll make me mutate into."

Enti and Bert sent gentle buffets of air towards the middle tower, as if hugging their rebellious friend, and surrounded him with gentle wordless pulse signals.

"We'll miss you." Bert's signal was slow and hesitant. "We've come a long way together."

Enti sent out a low hum of agreement and the three pulsed vision waves at each other for comfort until the Darkphase descended.

**

"Where the hell is that new reporter? I told him to have his article on my desk at 9am sharp. Someone fetch him in here *now*."

The editor's office door would have slammed shut had it not bounced off a young man with slicked back hair and an anxious expression who was running, straightening his tie, and arranging his papers at the same time.

"Sorry, Chief, sorry I'm late, my car broke down. Here's the article. I hope it's what you wanted."

"Car broke down," scoffed the editor. "You should use a push bike, like I do, much better for the environment. More green." He roared with laughter and the gaggle of journalists gathered around the doorway to watch the newbie get what was coming to him laughed sycophantically. The Chief drove a gas-guzzling Bentley and his latest editorial containing slanderous and fantastical accusations against those he called the "knit-your-own-hemp-sandals, tree-hugging-brigade" had caused questions to be asked in Parliament.

The young man smirked nervously as his new boss perused the closely typed pages.

"Wind turbines inhabited by an alien race. . . . Mind-bending thought waves. . . . Green campaigners influenced by a group of powerful beings from outer space. . . ."

The rising titter from outside the office was silenced as the editor slammed the papers down on the desk.

"Ben Turi," the big man roared, "you're a man after my own heart. Welcome on board!"

Andrea Gilbey

Just Desserts

"Then Henry VIII deactivated the monastarries because the monks and nuns wouldn't let him marry Anne Seymour. . . ." I shook my head and got busy with the red biro. I'd been right to get the year nine books over with at the beginning of the holiday: it was soul destroying. Had they listened to anything I'd said in class?

Brrrriiing!

Saved by the bell. I laid down my pen, pushed the stack of exercise books to the other end of the breakfast bar and reached for the phone. The display screen read "Dad - Home".

"Hi, Pops, how's it going?"

"Not bad, son, not bad." He paused.

"So what have you been up to this week?"

I reached for the coffee pot and poured another mugful, knowing that I might as well sit back and relax.

Dad rambled on, about winning a tenner on a scratch card and giving half of it to the kid who brings his newspapers, about the crossing supervisor outside the school next to his house and what the hell she drags around in that blasted shopping trolley, about the long-haired layabout who spends his nights in a sleeping bag on the bench outside the launderette and his days chatting up some blonde girl, and then the juicy bit of news—

"Eleanor Rigby must've died."

Her name wasn't really Eleanor Rigby, but that's what Dad called her, the rich old woman in the big Victorian house across the road. No-one had caught a glimpse of her for years, but occasionally you would see the lacy nets at her upstairs window twitch.

"There was a great big hearse out there, and a really fancy coffin, but it doesn't look like she had any family. There was just that companion-secretary woman who's so full of herself, and some bloke in a suit, but he didn't look that upset, so probably just her executor or something."

"I wonder who'll buy that old place," I mused. "It'll need some doing up, cost a fair bit of money to get that straight. She hasn't done anything with it for years."

There was a silence at the end of the phone that told me that the main point of this call was yet to come.

"On the subject of money. . . ." Dad paused.

"Go on," I encouraged him, trying to keep my voice neutral.

"I've had a letter, says it's from a solicitor, but I'm worried it might be one of them spam things again." His voice shook.

My mental red pen was drawing a line through "spam" and writing "scam" above it as my heart rate rose and my palms turned clammy. Dad had been caught by a door-to-door scammer a couple of years ago, promising a new driveway at bargain prices, and had been taken for all he had, plus a lot of what I had, too, which was why a forty-five-year-old assistant head teacher was living in a one-bedroom flat.

Not again.

"What do they want?" I asked, hating the hard tone in my voice but unable to control it.

"I'll read it to you." He cleared his throat and read in a monotonous drone.

Dear Mr Barker,

I am instructed on behalf of my client to invite you to attend an all-expenses-paid lunch at Uptown Tapas at 1pm on Wednesday July 27th.

I cannot at this time elaborate further, but if you attend the lunch you will find it to your financial advantage.

If you have any further questions, please feel free to contact me at . . .

blah, blah, blah,

yours sincerely,

F. Hardisty on behalf of Hardisty and Wilman Solicitors.

What do you think?" he asked nervously.

"Hang on a minute." I opened the laptop and typed in the name of the solicitors. "It's a real company. Give me that direct line number again, I'll give them a call in the morning; we'll soon find out if this is genuine or not."

***

"Frank Hardisty."

"Oh, good morning, Mr Hardisty, my name is James Barker, I'm Eric Barker's son."

"Yes?" The voice betrayed no sign of recognition.

"Um, I know about client confidentiality and all that, but my dad received a letter from you, inviting him to lunch on Wednesday. He's a bit concerned. He's in his seventies and, well, you never know these days, do you?" The other end of the line was silent. "I just wanted to check that the letter was genuine...." I tailed off.

"I understand your concern, Mr Barker, and I can assure you that the letter is perfectly genuine and no harm will come to your father. I myself will be hosting the lunch. I'm afraid I'm not authorised to allow your father to bring a friend or relative, but if you were to happen to be lunching at the same restaurant at the same time, that would be a happy coincidence, wouldn't it?"

"It would," I replied, catching on. "And the tables are quite close together there, I believe?"

"They are, indeed." I could hear a smile in the other man's voice. "I look forward to meeting your father on Wednesday. If you have no further questions. . . ?"

"Er, no, no, I don't. Thank you for your help. Goodbye."

"Goodbye. Oh, and I recommend the *patatas bravas*."

***

We were ten minutes early, of course we were. If Dad wasn't ten minutes early he considered himself late — it had been the only bone of contention between him and Mum in forty years of marriage.

"She'll be late for her own funeral," he always said, and, thanks to roadworks in the town centre, she was. Repeating his forty-year-old joke had probably been the only thing that kept him going that day.

"*Señors*, come in, come in," the waiter beamed, taking Dad's elbow to help him over the step.

"Table for one for Barker," I said, as the man collected up two menus, "and my dad has a lunch appointment with a Mr Hardisty."

"Your table is here, Sir." He indicated a single table against the wall. "And Sir, this is Mr Hardisty's." He pulled out a chair from under a table set for four people and ushered Dad into his seat. Dad glanced anxiously at the other place settings and looked at me for reassurance.

"I'll be right here with my book." I smiled. If the person seated opposite Dad started any trouble I'd be able to wrestle them into submission without getting up from my chair, the tables were so close together.

I settled myself with my book and a coffee and chose a selection of tapas while the waiter brought Dad a carafe of water and some bread. Dad had rearranged his cutlery twice and read the menu from cover to cover four times before the door buzzer sounded again and a small dapper man in a grey suit entered the restaurant.

"Mr Barker?" Both of us looked up, and Dad rose to shake hands, "I'm Frank Hardisty, good of you to come. Have you ordered yet?"

"Er, no, I thought I'd wait till everyone's here." Dad glanced at the other place settings. "Looks like it's a party!"

"All will become clear," smiled Mr Hardisty. "Please sit down."

I buried my nose in my book again, with one ear cocked to listen to the mundane weather conversation at the next table.

A young couple in the window were chatting quietly about their holiday, and I tried to tune them out so I could concentrate on whatever went on at the central table. The door buzzer sounded again and to my surprise in walked the young dreadlocked man who made his home on the bench outside the launderette.

"Mr Harris?" Frank Hardisty stood up, smiling, and shook the young man's hand. After a moment's hesitation Dad rose halfway from his seat and nodded at the newcomer.

Mr Hardisty made introductions and the young man sat down in the seat closest to my table, laying a large and rather tatty book down beside his place. I'm the kind of person who will read the label on a sauce bottle rather than have nothing to read, so I craned to see the title of the book and was taken aback to see my own name scrawled across the cover of an old psychology textbook.

The cheeky sod! I'd kept all my college books and stored them at my parents' house until just a few months ago when I'd decided to have a clear out. Most had gone to charity shops, but a few, including the one on the table across the aisle, were so heavily annotated that I'd just flung them in Dad's paper recycling box. This lad must have been digging around in there for something to read. Kudos to him if he could make head or tail of it; psychology had been my least favourite area of study.

The three men at the table cycled round the weather conversation again, interrupted by a crash at the door as a short, dumpy woman burst in, trailing a tartan shopping bag on wheels.

"Mrs Paxton—" Frank Hardisty started his welcome speech but was abruptly silenced as the woman ran her wheels over his foot.

"Oh! I'm so sorry, I just . . . oh, yes, thank you, it'll be fine there, no, really, so long as it's not in your way. . . ." The three diners, helped by the waiter, gently removed the trolley from her grasp and lodged it behind the counter as she settled herself in her chair and hid her embarrassment behind her menu.

"I'll just quickly run through the introductions again. I'm Frank Hardisty of Hardisty and Wilman, this is Kieran Harris," the young man nodded at his companions, "Eric Barker," Dad mumbled a greeting through his bread roll, "and Sandra Paxton." The stout lady, now more composed, beamed and gave a small side to side wave, her fingers stiff, hand moving from the wrist.

She leaned forward and asked the question that all of us wanted answered.

"Excuse me, but what are we all doing here? I mean, it's lovely and that, and very kind of you, Mr Hardisty, but why? My Barry didn't want me to come," she went on. "It could be a trap, he said, but as I said to him, who'd kidnap me? Anyway, he couldn't just take the day off, you know what they're like up at that factory, so he won't know whether I came or not, will he?"

Kieran Harris laughed and patted her arm.

"Whatever it is, we're all in it together, love, don't you worry."

"There's nothing for anyone to worry about, and all will become clear in due course," smiled Hardisty. "In the meantime let's eat, then we can talk over coffee."

The food was ordered to the accompaniment of fluttery giggles from Mrs Paxton at her own exaggerated Spanish pronunciation — "Me and Barry go to Marbella every year and we love Spanish food." — and the diners settled to eat in companionable silence, all eager to move on to coffee and the answer to the mystery.

＊

The chink of coffee spoons mingled with muttered conversation as the threesome at the centre table readied themselves to hear why they had been called together. I raised a finger to beckon the waiter and ordered a half carafe of red wine, settling back with my arms folded, abandoning any pretence of reading my book and now openly eavesdropping. Frank Hardisty caught my eye and smiled understandingly. He opened his briefcase and pulled out an official-looking document that instantly silenced the chatter at the table and made his three guests sit up straighter.

"I know you're all wanting to know why I asked you to come here, so I won't waste any more of your time. I am here to represent my client, the late Miss Rebecca Rowse."

I could see Dad looking blank, and guessed that Kieran's expression was the same from his immobile back, but Sandra Paxton piped up.

"Oh, the poor lady. You know the one, Eric." Sandra reached across to tap Dad's arm. She was the kind of woman who touched people a lot, and referred to everyone, even T.V. newsreaders and presenters, by their first names whether she knew them or not. "The old lady in the big house opposite you. She died a couple of weeks ago."

"Oh, Eleanor Rigby, you mean."

Frank Hardisty flashed him an appreciative glance, and Kieran Harris nodded and laughed. "Good name! I spoke to the secretary woman a few times, but never saw the old lady."

"Miss Rowse was a wealthy woman," continued Hardisty, "but she had no family. She has left large bequests to local charities, and . . ." he paused and glanced around the table, "she has left fifty thousand pounds to each of you."

The men gasped and Sandra Paxton squeaked.

"Fifty thous. . . each?" She sat back in her chair, arms limp at her sides, mouth gaping.

"But why?" Dad frowned. "I don't think I've spoken to her in years, and then it would only have been to pass the time of day."

"Yeah, why us?"

"I can let Miss Rowse tell you that in her own words. Would anyone like any more coffee, or maybe something a little stronger?" Hardisty's eyes twinkled as he made the offer.

"Let's have a jug of sangria," suggested Sandra, "to toast poor Miss Rowse, and to celebrate a little bit, too." She waved enthusiastically at the waiter.

"I will read what Miss Rowse had to say about all of you, if everyone is happy with that?" The three looked at each other and shrugged.

"In for a penny, in for fifty grand," grinned Kieran.

"Very well then. This is what Miss Rowse wrote."

There are three local people to whom I would like to leave bequests; all of whom have done good to their neighbours without realising that they were observed by the bedridden old lady in the big house. My secretary has all the details, but I will set forth here the reasons why I wish these three people to be rewarded.

Sandra Paxton, the local crossing supervisor. Not only is

she a kind and friendly person who does her job willingly, rain or shine, but she also undertakes to do daily shopping for three local pensioners, as well as taking their washing to the launderette, and I suspect subsidising both out of her own purse.

Sandra interlaced her fingers and looked down at her glass, her cheeks flushing. Kieran nudged her.

"So that's why you're in and out of the launderette all the time! I thought you must have, like, fifteen kids or something!"

"It's nothing much, really," Sandra mumbled. "I'd like to hope someone would do the same for me one day if I ever needed it. Let's hear about Kieran." She gave the young man's hand a squeeze.

Kieran Harris, a young man who is clearly intelligent and educated but has fallen on hard times. I know he reads anything and everything he can get his hands on to try to better himself; he always has a kind word for passers-by, and is willing to help carry heavy bags, but I am aware of one particular kindness. One day I saw a young blonde girl running down the street, in tears. This young man stopped her and asked what was wrong and they sat and talked on his bench for over an hour. The girl went on her way in a calmer frame of mind, but came back every day for two or three weeks and spent time sitting and talking to the young man and I could tell from her manner that she grew happier with every visit. I was intrigued and asked my secretary to arrange a seemingly chance meeting with the girl in a coffee shop and enquire casually about the young man. It appears that on the day I first saw the girl she had received some very bad news and was thinking about running away and leaving her job, her home, her friends, maybe even ending her life. Kieran took time to talk to her about his own experiences and made her see that her life could be turned around. She has since found a new job and re-built her life.

Three Finger Exercises

Kieran said nothing for a few minutes, but I could see his clenched hands shaking, then he looked up with a wobbly smile and spoke unsteadily.

"I only said to her what I wish someone had said to me when I was younger. She had the sense to listen, which is more than I would have done." He laughed softly. "With this money I can get myself back on my feet. I want to go to college and study psychology, become a counsellor or social worker." He patted the tatty old book on the table beside him. "Now, what did Miss Rowse have to say about Eric here?" The younger man grasped Dad's hand and held it tight. I gripped my own hands tightly together, wondering what was coming next.

Mr Hardisty smiled and resumed reading.

Eric Barker, my neighbour across the street, is not one to complain, and always has a pleasant greeting for his neighbours, but I can see that life has not been kind to him in the last couple of years. He is not a man of wealth, but has shown a great generosity in a small way. There was a little boy from the school next door to Mr Barker's house who runs errands for him. Every day, I watch the lad run to the corner shop and come back with two newspapers and a magazine, and Mr Barker gives him the money for them. The next day, the boy comes with more papers and a magazine and Mr Barker goes back into his house, puts the bundle down, and returns with the previous day's magazine, which he gives to the boy. I'm afraid I am a very nosy old woman, and I had my secretary arrange another "chance" meeting with this young lad in the corner shop. The magazines the boy was buying were football magazines. The young lad said he couldn't afford to buy them as his mother had two other children as well as him to bring up and couldn't spare pocket money, but Mr Barker always passed them on to him once he'd read them.

Andrea Gilbey

I choked on my wine at that point. Dad? Football magazines? His idea of sport was a game of darts at the pub. I doubted he even knew how many players were in a football team.

"It's just pennies here and there, and the lad deserves something for his trouble, he's a good kid, fetching the papers for me," Dad cleared his throat and avoided my eyes.

"So what will you do with the money, Eric?" asked Kieran.

Dad looked up, not at anyone around his table, but straight at me.

"I've got a few debts I need to clear, and I know another good lad who deserves a treat or two," he raised his glass, and I saluted him back with mine, smiling as we drank each other's health.

"What about you, Mrs Paxton?" asked Mr Hardisty, "what will you do with your money?"

The lady puffed out her cheeks.

"Well, I'll make sure my ladies are all right before I do anything, but my Barry retires in a year's time, and with our pensions and this inheritance we'll have enough to do what we've always dreamed of, sell up and move to Spain. I think you must be the teensiest bit psychic, Frank, choosing a Spanish restaurant to give us the news."

The merry bunch around the table broke up in laughter as glasses were raised and toasts made to futures that looked much brighter than they had just an hour before.

Three Finger Exercises

The Peace Bringer's Crossing

"Captain, signal to the vanguard to descend to one thousand atmons and prepare for landing."

"But Lady, this place looks hostile."

The tall woman faced at him squarely, her orange-flecked brown eyes firm. He lowered his gaze instinctively, brought up from infancy to avoid looking directly at the Sky-Ruler On Earth, just as one may not gaze at the Being itself without being blinded.

"And that is why we must land there."

She knew she had no need to say more. The man bowed his head sharply, raised his arms in front of his face in a precise and correct clenched-fisted crossed-wrist salute, and bounded athletically up the wooden steps to the wheelhouse of the gondola.

Samarah watched him go and an amused smile flickered across her face. She turned back to the prow of the ship and gripped the rail tightly, noting absently how taut the veins and sinews in the backs of her hands became. Landing was always tense, however many thousand times she had ordered it.

The blare of the horn from the wheelhouse alerted the two lead vessels, and the captain of the foremost ship gave the "We hear" signal with the on-board mirrors.

Flashes above Samarah's head, even brighter than the light surrounding the vessels, transmitted her order to the lead craft and she watched as the burners flared then dimmed in the first canopy, then the second, then she recognised the familiar but not unpleasant sinking feeling as the royal gondola started its descent.

Her cousin the captain was back at her side almost silently. From the corner of her eye she could see the muscle in his jaw bulge as he clenched his teeth.

"Captain?"

She tried again in a softer tone,

"Pantep?"

"Samarah, one of these missions will be one ocean crossing too far for you, you realise that, don't you?"

She shrugged.

"What choice do I have?"

She shielded her eyes with her arm to turn her face up towards the Sky-Ruler.

"You cannot force the whole of creation to follow our ways," Pantep growled impatiently.

She looked at him sideways, and he stared back, risking a royal reprimand.

"I must try," she said calmly.

***

The land rising from the icy sea ahead was grey and barren, with a coating of snow on the highest points. From the heart of it rose a slate tower of three concentric baileys, the topmost and centre tower showing sudden metallic flashes at the window ports. Weapons? In any case, it seemed that the inhabitants had seen the advancing travellers.

The three vessels descended silently, but although the air around the royal gondola was warm, the sea ahead stayed grey and cold, and the protective orb of golden sunlight surrounding the small procession grew smaller and smaller.

Samarah frowned. That shouldn't be happening. The royal fleet's power was having no effect on the atmosphere of this place.

Pantep fidgeted uneasily at her side.

"They must have some kind of . . . invisible wall around this place," he mused.

Samarah laughed, but the laugh sounded unconvincing even to her. She knew why Pantep was even more uptight than usual — in charge of the lead ship was his daughter, Cordavah, on her first mission as captain. Samarah had shown great confidence in her young cousin's abilities by awarding her command of the vanguard.

The lead gondola splashed down into the waves, the crew running around on the flight deck like busy insects to gather up the canopy before it hit the water. A salt water soaked canopy was a lethal problem when combined with the gas and fire needed to inflate it for the homeward journey.

A ramp was being lowered from the rocky island and signs of activity at the opening it revealed suggested that a greeting vessel was being launched. Samarah held out her hand, knowing even before she did so that her captain would have her viewing glass ready. She lined up the sights and adjusted the position of the lenses along the bronze rod. The people climbing into the boat — two, no, three of them — were dressed in baggy grey trews and black long-sleeved tunics, with their feet encased in heavy, shapeless boots. She scanned their faces intently for signs of aggression, but the faces looked blank and dull. Maybe that was their aggressive expression?

The royal gondola rocked as it hit the water and for few seconds the escort vessel was out of sight behind the waves. Samarah steadied herself and re-focussed her glass, watching as her young cousin made gracious gestures of introduction and thanks to the greeting party and stepped confidently into the small barge, accompanied by her landing party. The lead vessel sailed out of view behind the rocky land to find a mooring and the second ship glided forward to be met by another escort barge. Samarah straightened her white linen dress and smoothed her hair.

***

"Your Excellency, may I present the Lady Samarah," Cordavah intoned slowly and respectfully, her words coming through clouds of icy vapour. She gestured to her older cousin without looking directly at either her or the motionless elderly woman seated on the hard chair in the echoing chamber. The girl's meaning was clear, but the host's translator dutifully interpreted in an expressionless tone of voice.

The seated women spoke in the same toneless manner. The translator bowed, once to his mistress, and again to the visitors, his hands tucked into the opposite sleeves of his tunic.

"Citizen Hallvana welcomes you and asks you your purpose in visiting our community," he droned.

Samarah slid her arms from her unaccustomed warm cloak to make a salute, hurriedly tightened it around her shoulders once more, and spoke directly to the enthroned figure.

"Madam, we are peace bringers. We come from a society that has no war, no violence, no misery, no poverty. For centuries we have travelled to share our peace and light with the world. This is my duty as Sky-Ruler On Earth, and we are here to bring warmth to your country."

The interpreter had moved to stand behind his leader's chair and murmured a translation into the woman's ear. The leader's face remained stony.

Samarah continued,

"As we approached, we noticed that our light and warmth were unable to affect your climate. Is there. . . ." she hesitated, unsure how to put her question tactfully, "is there some deep sadness in this place?"

As the interpreter spoke, Hallvana's attendants took slow steps closer to the throne, as though protecting their leader. Samarah's landing party did not move, but she could feel waves of warmth and happiness emanating from them, pushing gently against their hosts' cold hostility.

The man stood watching his mistress, waiting for her to give him words to translate, but instead, Hallvana stood and faced Samarah.

"I speak your language . . . a little," she said with a slight bow. She straightened her back and looked directly into Samarah's face with a stare that held dignity and anger.

"Our lives are not yours to amend. We have lived this way for all time. What right have you to impose your ways on us?"

Something in the back of Samarah's mind itched. Where had she heard those words earlier?

"We bring you nothing but good," she replied, forcing a warm smile through chattering teeth. "Our forebears learned the secret of eternal and boundless peace and happiness and we wish to share it." She held her arms out in a gesture of giving, and immediately regretted it, feeling the cold of the chamber bite at her bones.

Hallvana's face flickered and her body tensed. Anger? No, Samarah realised, this was fear! Fear? Of happiness?

"We cannot change," the old woman said, harshly. "How can peace and happiness dwell here, in this hard, cold place? You know nothing."

A movement in the corner of her eye distracted Samarah. Cordavah was walking towards one of the grey-clad attendants, her arms outstretched, and a smile on her face of utter joy and welcome. Samarah felt a flicker of annoyance. Did the girl not feel the cold? Wait . . . she was cold and becoming angry — the place was starting to affect her.

"We must leave!" she cried, whirling round, wide-eyed, to face Pantep. "This place is dangerous."

Pantep's eyes were fixed on his daughter.

"Wait," he whispered, "watch."

Three Finger Exercises

Cordavah approached the young attendant and took her hands.

"You are young. You can change and learn to be happy. Come with us."

The grey-clad girl resisted slightly, then a slow smile spread across her face. Her whole body relaxed and a glow of light appeared around the two girls. A gasp arose from the room.

Hallvana shouted harsh words and the girl pulled her hands sharply out of Cordavah's grasp, slinking back into the shadows.

"We leave, now!" cried Samarah, sweeping towards the door, her brain reeling, trying to process what had just happened.

"Lady," Cordavah ran after her. "Cousin, please, we can't just give up!"

"I said, we leave!" Samarah's voice cracked as her shoes tapped across the stone floor.

Hallvana spoke again and four attendants detached themselves from her retinue and moved towards the door. Samarah drew herself up to her full regal height, but the attendants held back and motioned the visitors to pass ahead of them out of the room. A farewell escort.

Samarah watched as Cordavah gave the order to fire the burners and fill the canopy. She still felt cold. She leaned back against the railing of the wheelhouse and folded her arms. She had seen the doubting look in Pantep's eyes when she announced that she would travel back with Cordavah to monitor her command skills and knew that her cousin had seen through her. She also knew that his insistence on rigid protocol would never allow him even to think "I told you so" in front of her attendants.

Andrea Gilbey

As the gondola rose smoothly into the steadily warmer air she shed her cloak and strolled out onto the sunny main deck. The canopy's bright silk billowed as the hot air lifted it up and away from the cold, forbidding island. She took a deep breath and closed her eyes, allowing the peace and warmth from the Sky-Ruler to re-centre her, and felt her disturbance melt away.

She heard Cordavah's soft footsteps behind her but resisted turning to welcome the girl. What was the matter with her?

Cordavah cleared her throat softly.

"Lady? Cousin Samarah? I'm sorry if I overstepped a line. I was wrong."

Samarah turned. Her young cousin was standing with her head bowed, arms in the salute position but pointing downward, the most formal sign of respect and submission.

Samarah glided forward and wrapped her arms around the girl.

"No, you were right, I was wrong. But . . . Cordavah, I'm no longer young; maybe my powers are weakening. I was . . . afraid down there."

Cordavah started to protest, but Samarah hushed her.

"You are my heir and will one day be the Sky-Ruler On Earth. Today you have shown yourself truly worthy, and I . . . I have learned an important lesson. Our mission will continue, as it must, but it will be in safe hands without me. I can retire. Perhaps this was a good crossing after all." She pulled back and grinned at her young cousin.

"Of course your father won't be happy."

They laughed as the older woman took the girl's hand and led her to the railing to watch their warm, peaceful land come into view once more.

The Peacebringer's Crossing was previously published in Volume 20 of the Indian Creek Anthology Series, XX: SIW GOES PLATINUM, 2016

Three Finger Exercises

Andrea Gilbey

Double Digging

"Does anyone have any more to add to the minutes?" Myrna peered over her half-moon glasses and glanced around the table.

Debbie shook her head and drew a wriggly line under the last note on her pad, ending the line with a scribbled rose. Other heads shook around the table and a few voices muttered, "No," or "Nothing from me." A tuneless rhythmic breathy noise came from the seat on Debbie's left as her neighbour whistled silently through the gap in his teeth.

Myrna swept her gaze around the table once more, studiously avoiding eye contact with Malcolm, who was well known for being pedantic about points of order, and had once tried to waste a whole meeting in a debate about whether Myrna should be addressed as "Madam Chairman", "Madam Chairwoman" or just plain "Chair." On that occasion the lady in question had put a firm end to the discussion in her no-nonsense style.

"I'm not a man, last time I looked, I'm not a piece of furniture, I'm not a madam, and this is not the House of Commons. My name is Myrna, please call me by it."

Myrna signed her name at the bottom of the minutes sheet with a flourish, capped her fountain pen and pushed her papers to one side.

"Now, questions and tips. Who wants to start? Kaz?"

One of the society's newer members lowered the hand she had tentatively raised and smiled.

Three Finger Exercises

Debbie instinctively smiled back. She liked Kaz a lot. The girl's bleached blonde dreadlocks, nose ring and peace sign tattoos had caused some sniffiness among a few of the older members, but by sheer force of personality Kaz had won over the doubters, and was turning into a good gardener. Her immaculate allotment held neat rows of organically grown vegetables, though how she found the time to keep it so tidy while holding down a full time job and looking after her seven-year-old son was anyone's guess.

"I'm sure this is a real newbie question," she apologised, "but I'm having awful problems with black fly on my broad beans. Any ideas, please?"

A buzz of conversation started up around the table as all the members tried to put forward their own personal solution. Debbie turned to the silent man beside her.

"Steve, didn't you tell us you had won several classes with your broad beans?" she asked loudly enough to be heard over the babble. "How did you manage the black fly?"

Her neighbour flipped a lock of dark blond floppy hair away from his face and smiled a disarming smile, showing the gap in his teeth. As always, Debbie felt irritated at herself for finding him irritating. She secretly harboured an idea that the second newest member of the group thought himself endearing and adorable and was quite convinced that everyone else agreed with him.

"Well, I . . . I suppose it must have been the climate, or the area or something, but I didn't get black fly. Maybe I'm just lucky, hmm?" He winked chummily at Kaz, who stared stony-faced back at him for a frozen second, one eyebrow raised, then turned to the elderly man beside her. Debbie watched the girl's reaction interestedly. So she wasn't the only one who found him annoying.

"So, Dave, you think that will work?" Kaz was saying to the older man loudly. Dave adjusted his hearing aid with a piercing whistle and repeated the advice that he, and most of the rest of the group, had already given.

"I say weak soapy water, sprayed on them three times a day." He nodded sagely. Corner-wise across the table from him and slightly out of his eye line Babs grinned at Debbie and rolled her eyes.

"The oracle has spoken." Babs said in a stage whisper that Dave's hearing aid would never catch.

Myrna cleared her throat to call the assembly together again.

"Any more questions?" The heads shook again. "Then any hints or tips, anyone?" She saw by Dave's quizzical expression that he hadn't heard what she said. "Any tips?" she bawled.

"Buy new batteries," Steve sniggered. Debbie kicked him under the table.

"I've been working on a new tomato feed," announced Dave, "and I think I've found a really good recipe."

Pens were clicked all around the table as the members prepared to take down words of wisdom from their most experienced colleague. Steve shot his cuffs and sat up looking intent and Malcolm started a fresh page of his notebook, dating the page and writing in neat block capitals, "Dave's Tomato Feed" before ruling a double line under the words.

Dave proceeded to ramble his way through a recipe involving boiled nettles, alfalfa tablets, borage leaves, egg shells and cat hair while his friends made copious notes.

"And of course there's one special ingredient," he finished, winking and tapping the side of his nose. "It mustn't go any further than this room." He looked dramatically over his shoulders, right, then left, until Myrna's steely glare caught his eye. The group leader tapped her watch pointedly.

"It'll be poo," Babs muttered under her breath. "It's always poo."

Debbie stifled a giggle as Dave declaimed, "Rabbit . . . poo." He glanced in turn at Myrna, Debbie, Kaz and Babs with a slight old-fashioned bow before uttering the second word. Debbie wasn't sure whether to be flattered that he thought her enough of a lady to be protected from "naughty" words, or offended that he thought her too uptight to know them.

There being no more tips or ideas forthcoming, Myrna turned the subject to the upcoming Inter-Club produce show between the Fairbrook Horticultural Society and their main rivals, the society from the neighbouring village of Harpers Green.

"As we all know; Harpers Green have won the show cup for the last two years. Ted Buckland is determined to make it a hat trick this year, so we need to pull out something really special to get Fairbrook's name back on the cup. Divide and rule should be our strategy. We need as many entries in as many different classes as possible to stand a chance of winning the show trophy. I will be entering five classes, a Plate of Five Runner Beans, a Plate of Onions From Sets, a Basket of Kitchen Vegetables, a Plate of Tomatoes and the Heaviest Onion."

As she spoke she handed round lists of the available classes for entry.

"Whew!" Kaz puffed out her cheeks. "Five runner beans? Just five? There's no room for error there, is there!"

"Perfection is the only way to win," beamed Babs, running her eyes eagerly over the list. "I'll be entering my tomatoes as usual, and I'm hoping to have a nice crop of early whites this year, aaaannnd . . . shallots." She smiled around the table, already seeing her perfect vegetables lying smugly on a black velvet cloth.

"I will be entering my onions, as usual, in the Three Identical Onions class, and if my carrots are as good as last year I should be able to do well in the One Carrot No Shorter Than Seven Inches class," said Malcolm, writing his choices in his notebook in precise capitals and proceeding to draw a planting plan on a new blank page.

"Spuds for me," beamed Dave, "All the classes! And tomatoes." A dirt-ingrained finger ran down the list. "And I might have a punt at the Vase of Sweet Peas this year."

A respectful hush settled on the table. Ted Buckland was famous throughout the district for his tomatoes and sweet peas, so Dave's challenge would not go unnoticed, and should he win, it would be a great coup for the Fairbrook Society.

"I need to take this home and talk to Stuart when he gets back from his parent-teacher evening. I can't make any decisions without my head gardener," smiled Debbie, waving the list and tucking it into her notebook. "What about you, Steve? Which classes will you enter?"

"Oh, I don't know. . . ." He pouted and flicked his hair. "I've won pretty much all of these classes in the past so it's a hard decision." He gave the room the benefit of his gap-toothed smile. "I'll let you know." He shuffled his papers together and stood up.

Myrna, reclaiming her authority, stood up and collected her floral shopping bag.

"If we're all done then I'll see you next week at the same time. Goodnight, everyone."

**

As she drove home from work the next evening, Debbie's eye was caught by a tall figure with floppy hair standing by the side of the road talking to someone. She tooted her horn and flapped a hand out of the window with a smile, but when she looked in her rear view mirror the smile changed to a puzzled expression. The young man was talking animatedly to Ted Buckland, and in his hand was his notebook, the same notebook he had been writing in last night. She recognised the childish Batman cover. The two men were bending over the page, following the tip of Steve's pen as he pointed to a line in the book. Neither looked up at her toot.

***

"Hello, anyone home?" She threw her bag onto the kitchen table, making a draught that blew a piece of lined paper to the floor. Woodstock scuttled under the table after it and Debbie deftly scooped it away from the dog's claws as she walked to the sink to fill the kettle. While she waited for it to boil she read in Stuart's slanting scrawl, "Sorry Debs, I'll be late tonight, I forgot it's year nine parents' evening. Don't wait dinner if you're hungry. Love you."

She wasn't particularly hungry and after finishing her tea she looped Woodstock's lead from the coat rack and looked at him encouragingly.

The evening air was just a little chilly as the pair strode out across the downs. Woodstock romped on ahead, chasing rabbits, unaware that his frantic barking was giving them at least a five-minute warning to get away. Debbie balled her fists in the deep, baggy pockets of her aran cardigan, threw back her head took a deep lungful of the clear air.

Woodstock came gambolling back, barking, running around her in a tight circle and haring away again up the hill.

"What is it, boy, what are you showing me?" she panted as she followed him up the slope.

The dog was running towards a bent figure, who seemed to be scouring the ground for something.

"Hello! Lost a contact lens?" she called cheerily. "The times that's happened to me. . . ."

She stopped in confusion as the figure straightened up. It was Ted Buckland, his face flushed from stooping and embarrassment.

"Oh, hi, Debbie. I won't shake hands, I'm collecting, er. . . ." He indicated the polythene bag in his left hand.

Rabbit droppings? The image of this man and her gardening

colleague standing head to head over a notebook flashed into her head. Dave's recipe! The slimeball had shared Dave's tomato feed recipe with the rival club's chairman! Just wait till she got her hands on that little. . . .

Clenching her fists, she forced a smile.

"Each to their own." She laughed gaily. "Come on, Woodstock! Here, boy." She dug a tennis ball from her pocket and hurled it down the hill, running down after the excitable dog so fast that she almost tripped.

***

"So what do you think I should do?" she finished, through the last mouthful of garlic bread.

"Are you sure Steve was reading from his FHC notebook?" asked Stuart.

"Positive. It's weird enough that a grow man uses a child's Batman exercise book, why would he have two the same? I don't want to tell Myrna yet; I don't have any real proof, and you know how she worries about the slightest conflict in the group. I'll sleep on it and maybe talk to Babs tomorrow. There's plenty of time before next week's meeting."

Stuart nodded.

"Good idea. Babs has been in the society even longer than we have. She'll know how to handle this. I'll make sure I get away in time to come to the next meeting to see what this chap's up to."

***

After selling large letter stamps to someone who wanted second class regular letter stamps, sticking a Special Delivery label on upside down, and almost giving a holiday-maker dollars instead of Euros, Debbie realised that her mind wasn't on her job. In her head she was having imaginary confrontational conversations with Steve even though as yet she had no proof that anything underhand was going on. She frowned and tapped her nails on the counter as her last customer left the shop. Was it just that she instinctively didn't like the man? No, he was up to something, sure as eggs are. . . .

Eggs!

The doormat buzzer rudely interrupted her thoughts and she pulled herself together enough to check a passport form thoroughly, but once the customer left she let her thoughts go back to the trail of eggs. 4.30. The postman would be in to collect the day's mail in a few minutes and she could close the post office counter. If no-one came in for any groceries before the postman came she could maybe close up early . . . She nodded, answering her own unspoken question and picked up the phone.

"Fairbrook Library, Yvonne speaking, how may I help?"

"Vonnie, it's me. Have you got time to dig something out of the local rag archives before you close?"

"Debs, you sound quite breathless! What's the matter?"

"Oh, something and nothing, maybe, gardening club stuff, but I'm working on a hunch here; humour me, please. Would you be able to find the news reports on the Inter-Club show from '99? If you can hunt them out before closing time, I'll pop over as soon as I can. I think I know what I'm looking for."

"1999?" queried Yvonne. "Isn't that the year of the Great Egg Disaster? Are you sure you want to look back at that?"

"Yes," said Debbie firmly. "Can you find it?"

"Shouldn't take more than ten minutes."

"Good. I'll be over as soon as I've locked up."

Quickly, before another customer had a chance to open the door, she flipped the sign to "closed" and hurried through to the back office to make everything secure for the night. The red post van pulled up as she opened the front door to leave, and she bundled the post bags into the collection driver's arms, barely allowing him time to scan the collection point bar code.

"What's your hurry, Debbie, got a hot date?" The man grinned.

She ignored the comment and pushed him away from the door so she could bring down the shutter.

"See you tomorrow, Wayne."

The newspapers she had asked for were laid out neatly on a table in the study area of the library, and Yvonne was waiting, curious to know what the urgency was.

Debbie dropped her bag beside a chair and started leafing through the papers before she even greeted her friend.

"Vonnie, you're an angel, well done. Now then . . . No, not this one, must be in the Gazette. . . ."

She flipped pages, licking her finger to get a grip on the paper.

"Here!"

She stabbed at the page, pointing to a headline in large type above a photo of a man and a boy holding a trophy. "Eggstravaganza At Local Flower Show," the headline read.

Debbie stared at the photo. There was Ted Buckland, younger, slimmer and with more hair, and holding the other handle of the large silver cup he was grasping was a small boy with floppy blond hair and a gap between his front teeth.

Debbie read the article aloud, gabbling so fast that Yvonne could only catch one word in three, so she moved round to read over her friend's shoulder.

"Local grower Ted Buckland poses with the Inter-Club cup, assisted by his nephew, ten year old Stephen Peet. Buckland's best in show for his vase of spectacular sweet peas helped secure the club trophy for the Harper's Green Horticultural Society. The event was not without drama, as an accident involving prime clutch of goose eggs, entered by local post mistress Debbie Clark from the Fairbrook H.S., turned a close-run competition into a triumph for the visiting club."

Three Finger Exercises

"That's him!" exclaimed Debbie. "The kid who knocked the trestle table over and smashed all my eggs. I swear he did it on purpose, and he's still at it!"

"Have you been out weeding in the full sun again, Debs?" Yvonne's expression was bemused. "Who's still at what?"

Debbie stabbed again at the photo, poking the face of the grinning boy.

"Him. He's in our club, joined a few months ago. He reckons he's won cups and rosettes for just about anything you can grow, but he's living in a flat, allegedly borrowing a friend's garden, and has never once produced any evidence of anything he's grown, or even the slightest bit of dirt under his nails. The other day, I caught him showing his club notes to Ted Buckland. His uncle."

"So you think he's a mole? Gardening . . . mole . . . geddit?" Yvonne nudged her.

Debbie rolled her eyes.

"Very funny." She nibbled at her nails, thinking fast.

"Can I take a copy of this? I need to talk to some of the other club members. This . . . man . . . could completely sabotage our chances in the Inter-Club show."

Yvonne was already spreading the page on the glass of the photocopier.

"This is on the house," she said, as Debbie rummaged in her purse for a twenty pence piece to pay for the copy. "It'll be worth it if the Egg Smasher finally gets his comeuppance."

***

"Here they come." Babs nudged Dave and woke him up from an after-dinner snooze. Kaz jumped up from her deckchair and ushered Debbie into it, turning it slightly so the older woman was shaded by Dave's rows of runner bean plants. Stuart nodded to the other club members and perched on a large upturned flowerpot. They'd decided to meet on Dave's allotment, as it was quiet and they would hear anyone approaching, not that Debbie could now imagine that Steve had ever set foot on an allotment.

**

Babs handed Debbie a glass of her peapod wine and offered a plate of chocolate chip cookies.

"So come on then, spill the beans. Why all the secrecy?"

Debbie unfolded the photocopy and held it out to the others. She pointed to the boy in the picture.

"Recognise him?"

She told the story, starting with the saga of the smashed goose eggs for Kaz's benefit, and finishing with her sighting of Steve passing Dave's recipe to his uncle.

Kaz's eyes flashed and she balled her fists.

"He's a spy! Kick him out of the club!"

"We've no proof, Kaz," came the voice of reason from Stuart. "That's why we don't want to tell Myrna yet; she'll only worry. We need to watch him. He'll trip himself up sooner or later. That type always does."

"I've got a better idea," said Babs, grinning. "Let's set him up. Feed him something he can pass on, but make sure Harpers Green won't benefit from it."

Three faces lit up with delight at her suggestion. Dave looked from one to the other of them, as they all turned and smiled at him.

"Dave, get your recipe book out. Let's see what we can come up with."

**

"Any hints and tips?" asked Myrna. "The big day is only three weeks away, so the more knowledge we can share, the better we will do as a team." She beamed round the table at the members, encouraged by their reports of blooming plants and flourishing vegetables. She was confident that her own basket of kitchen vegetables would be a veritable cornucopia of deliciousness, she had so much produce coming to ripeness.

"I've worked on an improvement to my tomato feed." Dave pulled a sheaf of papers from a tatty carrier bag. "To save you all having to write it out again, Debbie's very kindly typed it up for me."

He peeled a sheet from the top of the pile, peered at the hand-written name on the document and passed it to Malcolm.

Debbie and Babs carefully avoided looking at each other or catching Kaz's eye. Typing the recipe and giving out individually named copies was Kaz's idea — with Malcolm and Myrna not in on the plot, it was the only way the bogus recipe could be fed to Steve without innocent parties using it by mistake. The three women and Stuart had carefully positioned themselves around the table so that there was no chance of Myrna or Malcolm catching a glimpse of Steve's copy and realising that it was different from theirs.

"Hmm, very interesting!" Steve studied the sheet of paper, nodding wisely. "I shall make sure I mix some up as soon as I get home, although my tomatoes really don't need it. They're turning into real beauties."

"I'll pop round tomorrow night and have a look at them," said Dave. "You're using your friend's garden down Brook Street, aren't you? Third house in from the top?"

"Er, yes, yes, I am," Steve stuttered, "but, um, it might not be convenient . . . er. . . ."

"It's ok, you don't have to wait in. I'll go along the back alley and peek over the fence," beamed Dave. "It's no trouble."

Steve smiled weakly.

✻✻✻

"That's four fifty-two, please, love . . . Oh, sorry, one moment . . . Fairbrook Post Office, Debbie speaking."

An excited voice hissed urgently in her ear.

"Debs he's here, the Egg Smasher, using the photocopier!" It was Yvonne.

"Can you see what he's copying?" asked Debbie.

"No, but the copier's low on paper, and I deliberately didn't fill it. If he makes more than a few copies, it'll stop and he'll have to call me over."

"Genius!" gloated Debbie. "Call me back in a bit." She waved her customer out and fidgeted at the counter, arranging and re-arranging gift cards, not wanting to move away from the phone. Her hand shot out to grab it at the first ring.

"Well?"

"It says "Dave's Tomato Feed — Revised Recipe," hissed Yvonne.

"Gotcha!" Debbie punched the air.

**

Stuart suddenly straightened up from loading the dishwasher.

"Oh, Debs, I've got something to show you." He pulled his phone from his pocket and swiped the screen. "I popped into the garden centre after school to get some cane toppers before you poke your eye out on those broad bean poles, and you'll never guess who I saw skulking around with a trolley full of tomato plants."

He handed the phone to his wife.

"Swipe through the gallery; there's a few. I had to zoom in from a distance so he didn't see me, but you can see who it is. More evidence."

Debbie nodded and smiled gleefully at her husband.

"And what do you bet he won't have the brains to take the labels off before Dave gets round there on his visit."

They hi-fived each other, laughing.

**

Three Finger Exercises

Myrna walked back to her place flushed and beaming, and fluttered her first-place ribbon at her club colleagues.

"Well done, Myrna." Debbie patted her leader's shoulder. "That basket is beautiful."

"It's neck-and-neck," said Myrna. "It's all down to the tomato classes and the Best In Show, and I think that's between your goose eggs and Malcolm's onions."

The group quietened as the judge approached the tomato tables. Every plate was heaped with glowing red fruit, and there was very little to choose between them in appearance.

"Good colour, nice and firm, and they smell. . ." the judge raised the plate to his nose and smiled, "wonderful!"

He cut the topmost fruit in half and the small crowd craned forward to see.

"Good firm flesh, nice thin skin, plenty of seeds. Let's taste . . . Mmm! Sweet and juicy, very good."

He moved along the table, cutting and tasting one fruit from each plate. The last plate on the Fairbrook table was Steve's. The judge commented on the glowing colour, shining skin and firm feel of the fruit, then cut into one.

"Oh dear. Oh dear, me, that's the worst case of blossom end rot I've ever seen. What a pity."

Debbie tried to keep her expression disappointed as she viewed the completely black insides of Steve's tomatoes. A gasp ran around the hall, and Ted Buckland took an involuntary step forward, glaring at the younger man, before he remembered that he wasn't supposed to know him, and stepped back, trying to look pleased that the rival club had done badly.

The judge moved to the Harper's Green table and started to examine the fruit. Every plate met with praise for its external appearance, but every fruit was black inside. Almost as black as Ted Buckland's angry face. His club members gathered around in surprise and anger, and voices were raised inside the huddle. Ted's head lifted and his suffused face looked around for his errant nephew, but the young man had gone without waiting to hear the final result.

The judge cleared his throat.

"Well, um, I think it's quite clear from that round that the winner of all the tomato classes is the Fairbrook society. Very well done, and commiserations, Harper's Green. Now for the final result, although from the scores, we already have a champion club."

He stepped back to the judging table and lifted the Best In Show shield.

"It was a very close-run thing, but the winner of this year's Best In Show is . . . the goose eggs."

A piercing two-fingered whistle rang out from the crowd at the back of the hall as Debbie stepped out to collect her trophy, waving it in salute to Yvonne, who let fly another shrill celebration.

"And the overall Inter-Club trophy goes to. . ." the judge raised his voice over the hubbub, "Fairbrook Horticultural Society."

"Where did Steve go?" asked a bemused Myrna, as her club-mates pushed her forwards to claim the cup.

"Don't worry about him," laughed Debbie, "I don't think we'll be seeing him again — he's gone, sure as eggs are eggs."

Double Digging was previously published in Volume 20 of the Indian Creek Anthology Series, XX: SIW GOES PLATINUM, 2016

Three Finger Exercises

Andrea Gilbey

The Legend of Zen Koi

A long, long time ago, in old Japan, there was a magical lake.

In the lake lived beautiful koi carp, of many different colours, with many different patterns in their scales.

The lake was magical because the supply of food for the koi never ran out.

As food was so abundant, the koi became greedy and ate everything they could find; flat fish; slim, fast-swimming fish; jellyfish of all kinds; hard, armour plated fish; flying fish; even the puffer fish that are so poisonous to most creatures were food to these koi.

The koi ate so much that they became fat and lazy. They stopped swimming across the lake to mate, and only mated with the fish who lived close by, so their patterns and colours became dull.

One day, King Carp became tired of the koi's behaviour, and he summoned them to a meeting under the waterfall at the head of the lake.

"I am disappointed in you," he thundered, thrashing the water with his tail. "You have become greedy, fat and lazy, and look at you — all of you who live in the same part of the lake look the same. You need to be more balanced, more Zen. I can see that I must give you some rules to live by.

"From now on, your food is limited. You may only eat so many of each species, and you must eat just that number — no less and no more. Only once you have eaten your share of the poorer fish can you move on to the richer species. If you are slow and hungry, you may find a special flower that contains a jewel. If you swallow the jewel, it will give you energy to swim faster and find food.

"You must also travel to mate. You may no longer mate with a koi that looks like yourself."

One of the koi spoke up.

"Oh great King Carp, what happens when we have eaten all the food we are allowed?"

"What happens to all living things? You die, and move on to a higher existence.

"When you have no more food to eat, you will leap from the lake, higher than you have ever leapt before, over the arch of the sky-pond and into the great fireball, where you will become a dragon and live for all eternity."

**

And that is why, if you sit by a pool on a summer's day, you will see koi carp jumping from the water. Some say they are merely catching flies, but now and then, one koi will jump higher than it has ever jumped before, and transcend mortal life to become a dragon, and live for ever more.

The Short Straw

1942

My name's Alf, but most people call me Elf, partly because that's how "Alf" sounds in North London where I grew up, and partly because I'm so small.

I've always been small. There were some kids who had a sudden growth spurt when their hormones caught up with them, and some who were taller than the rest but then stopped growing, but not me. My dad used to tell me to go and stand in the muck heap to see if it made me grow.

I was always in the front row of the school photograph, always the one who was hoisted up on a roof or shoved through a window to rescue a ball, always the one climbing up on someone else's back to put the classroom clock an hour fast, the one who had to go under the floorboards to rescue my sister's pet mouse.

"Go on, Elf, you first, you're the smallest."

Story of my life, really.

I suppose you could say it's being small that landed me here.

***

I wanted to be a jockey - had dreams of winning the Derby, the Gold Cup, the Grand National, but the war put a stop to that before I even had a chance to try for an apprenticeship or anything.

I joined up as soon as I could, in the Airforce. I was only just seventeen, but I lied through my teeth at the recruiting station and puffed my chest out at the medical. I wanted to be in at the beginning and I wanted to choose where I went. I didn't fancy all that square bashing and rolling around in muddy trenches, although they say this war isn't like the last one, not so hand-to-hand.

No, I wanted to fly. When you're in the air it doesn't matter how small you are. Once you're in that cockpit and up above the clouds, you can see the whole world down below you. Master of all you survey, and all that.

Mum wasn't happy about me joining up, but I think she was more upset that I'd told a lie than at the thought that I might get killed. Dad couldn't say anything: he'd run away from home at sixteen to join up the last time around.

The training suited me. I was always quick and nimble, good at PT, and quite a fast runner, even with my short legs. Nippy, like.

I wanted to be a fighter pilot, but I couldn't take all that twisting and turning in the air — G-force, they call it. They sent me up with an instructor and I threw up all over him and the inside of the plane at the first barrel roll. The doc said it's something to do with my ears that affects my balance, so no dog fights for me. I've got my suspicions that my accent didn't suit either. Can't have a north London boy mixing with the public school chaps in the officer's mess, what? My old school tie was usually used to hold my shorts up.

So they put me in Bomber Command. And guess what? They've got the perfect job for short-arses like me — tail-end Charlie. The rear gunner in a bomber. I got myself posted onto a Lancaster, best plane in the world, in my opinion.

The rear gunner's tucked away in a little glass bubble at the back of the plane, with almost a three-hundred-and-sixty-degree view of the world. You've got the comms. in your ears, of course, you can hear all the commands and directions, but you're on your own in there, easy to concentrate and stay focussed, so long as you don't mind heights, that is.

I soon got used to it, being suspended over thousands of feet of empty air. It's smashing in daylight, flying home at sunrise after a night sortie — you really get to appreciate how green England is, even with all the bunkers and concrete defences everywhere, and the parks ripped up to grow food — but at night it's something else. You head off on a bombing raid into almost complete blackness, so dark that you can hardly even spot your fighter escort, then you suddenly see tracer bullets whizzing past, or a flare of gunfire from the Ack Acks on the ground.

Occasionally it's a plane spinning down, wildly out of control, streaming fire. Whether it's one of ours or one of theirs, you hope the poor sods bailed out in time. Up there, we're all in the same boat, just doing our job.

It's odd really, all this talk of the Hun, and how bad the Enemy is, but when you see a pilot's eyes above his mask and you realise he's just a scared lad like you, it could be your brother in there, or your best mate from home. Terrible what war makes men do to each other, and none of us chose it.

Of course we thought we were invincible — you have to or you couldn't do the job. If you went up there expecting to be shot down and killed, if you even thought about it, you couldn't do it. Some lose their nerve, we're all human. They get put onto ground duties until they get over it. Some never get over it.

But we'd flown so many missions without so much as a scratch that when that German fighter shot our tail off and hit one of the engines we couldn't actually believe it had happened to us. There was no panic, just a sense of calm and a job to be done, try to land the old bus somewhere away from civilians and stay alive if possible. We'd had a good run, now we thought our number was up. They say your past life flashes in front of you, but mine didn't. All I could think of was the future I wasn't going to have. No kids, no home of my own, my wife, sister and parents never really knowing what happened to me or where I was buried.

Even this time, our uncanny luck held and we landed on water.

I must've been knocked out cold by the impact of landing. I've no recollection of what happened to the rest of the lads. The first thing I remember is asking where we'd come down and a German soldier telling me, "Im See!" I thought he was saying we'd landed in the sea, but apparently See is a lake. You live and learn.

***

So here we are, all still together, patched up, put to rights and imprisoned in Stalag . . . no, I'd better not write it here. I'll take this diary with me when we go. If I get out and away safely, I might be able to write a book about all this, make a name for myself. If not, the longer it takes them to find out where I've escaped from, the better chance the other lads will have of getting away.

I thought it short-sighted of them to put all of us together in one hut. I mean, we've been a team for three years, so we don't really have to talk to know what the rest are thinking. We're like brothers, we work as one man, so digging the tunnel, arranging forged papers, civvy clothes, all of that was just like a training exercise, a bit of fun to keep us occupied and get one over on Fritz. Naturally, as the smallest, I got the job of going down the tunnel and hauling out bucket after bucket of soil. I must have lost a good stone from the effort, and the food we're given here isn't exactly the kind of thing you'd get at the Ritz, not that I'd know.

Andrea Gilbey

And now it's real. We're actually going out, in just a couple more hours.

They wanted a volunteer to wake everyone up when the time comes, so I said I'd do it. "I don't need as much sleep as the rest of you," I said. "There's not so much of me." I knew I wouldn't sleep, anyway, too keyed up.

I'm writing this in the hut window, making the most of the searchlight every time it comes around, so that's why it's a bit scrappy, I have to keep pausing when the light turns away again.

At least if I'm caught and shot there's a chance that someone will find this and have the kindness to send it on to Doll so she'll know I tried to get home to her; know I was thinking about her.

I think about her all the time. We've only been married just over a year, got married while I was on a forty-eight-hour pass and that's all the time we had together. Not much of a honeymoon, two nights in her mum's back bedroom. I was hoping I might have left her with a little Alfred or Freda, but no. Maybe that's for the best, all things considered. Who knows what kind of world we'll have when all this is over.

People say we have to be positive, look forward to a better world, people it with children who'll appreciate what we went through to keep their freedom safe, but what if, just what if, we don't win? I don't want my kid growing up under the Nazis. So, like I say, maybe it's for the best that Doll didn't fall easily.

I've got our wedding photo in my wallet, against my heart, like. Bless her, she wore the flattest shoes she could find and even sagged at the knees a bit in the photos so she wouldn't tower over me. She's not overly tall or anything, a nice average size, just a comfortable armful, but in her bare feet she hits five foot six, and I'm only five two, even in my flying boots. The photo's a bit worn at the edges, but if — no, when — I get home, we'll do it again properly, have a church blessing and a slap-up reception with all our friends there and get proper photos taken in a studio.

I haven't heard from her since I've been in here. We've had Red Cross parcels, and some of the other lads have had letters from wives and girlfriends, but none for me.

I'm trying not to worry. Maybe she just didn't get the telegram saying I'd been captured.

Or maybe she's regretting . . . no. I won't write it. These thoughts prey on your mind in the early hours when there's nothing else to think about.

Two o'clock. Zero hour is 0300 hours, so I'll need to start waking the lads soon. We've got to put rolled up blankets in our beds and hope that when the guards come at five to check they don't look closely. Roll call isn't until seven. We should be nearly ten miles away by the time they notice we're missing.

This must be how they feel in the trenches, waiting to go over the top. Dad said it was the waiting that killed you, not literally, but I know what he meant, now. Going out on a mission is different; you've got a set job to do, checks to make, the same phrases to say, a routine that takes your mind off what you're going to do. Then once you're in the drop zone, you don't think, you just react.

This is a leap into the unknown. Who know whether we'll even make it outside the perimeter. And then what? We don't even know where we are really, will we make it to neutral territory? By this time tomorrow we could be on our way home, we could be back here in solitary, or we could be dead.

The lads are stirring; some sixth sense is telling them it's nearly time. I must close here and get ready. See you on the other side, dear diary, God willing.

Andrea Gilbey

One thing's for sure, I know what Bill, our captain, will say once those floorboards are lifted under his bed.

"Go on, Elf, you first, you're the smallest."

***

2002

I'm glad I brought my hip flask with me, it's a bit nippy standing around waiting. Drinking on parade! We'd never have got away with that back then, but everyone's got a little tot of something to keep them warm. Well, it is November, after all.

Funny, finding this little notebook after all these years, tucked away with my medals. I never look at them, haven't opened that box in years, and I don't really know what made me come here this year. I've always watched the parade on the telly, never thought about coming, but now . . . well, there's hardly any of us left. I felt I should make the effort.

Anyway, Doll, I promised I'd write down everything that happens so you can read it when I get back. I wish you could be here, but you wouldn't be able to hear the music, and that's what's giving me the shivers. Funny how a military band always makes the hair on the back of my neck stand up, even though they're so far away I can hardly hear them. We all stood silent for the service, but couldn't really hear anything except the big drum when they played Nimrod, everything was so distorted over the speakers.

We're almost right at the back of the parade, as we should be, the Rear Gunners' Association bringing up the rear, can't even see the Cenotaph above all the people. Sally and Jason must be somewhere in the crowd. I'm glad the boy could come and see his old grandad marching; I might not do this again. I hope they've found a spot at the front where he can see. He's going to be another short-arse like me by the look of him.

Three Finger Exercises

We've got a bit of a wait before we march off, so everyone's milling about talking; no need to form up until we get the nod from the section commander or whoever he is, the chap with the clipboard. He's enjoying himself having one more chance to be the big I Am; he's probably an ex RSM.

One of the old crew's here, Chalky White. He was the radio operator. Says there's only the two of us left now. Of course, Harry never even made it back home, got septicaemia when he gashed his leg in the tunnel. We should have made him stop and get it treated, even if we were captured again, but he wouldn't have it, he was all for getting away, over the border into Switzerland, and by the time we got there it was too late for him. They took his leg off below the knee, but it was gangrenous and it spread, poor old bugger. The only consolation was that he was too delirious by the end to know what was happening.

Horrible, that was, and then going to see his wife and little girl when I came home, telling them he'd died.

***

People watch The Great Escape and think it was all camaraderie and excitement, but it was mostly dirt, fear, darkness and damp. I hid in a drainpipe one night, and it rained like the second Flood was coming. I didn't dry out for a week.

Reading back over what I wrote that night when we escaped, it seems like a lifetime ago, like it happened to someone else.

I never showed you this little diary, did I, love? Never wrote that best-selling book, either. Once I got home, I just wanted to forget all about it, especially when Sally came along all those years later, just when we thought we'd never have children: that was like a new start for us, wasn't it?

We've been lucky, really. Apart from your hearing, we're both still going strong — sound in wind and limb, as they say.

Andrea Gilbey

**

It looks like we'll be moving off any minute; the chap with the clipboard's bustling around getting people formed up in ranks, so I'd better put this away. I'll finish it on the train on the way home and tell you all about the parade. Maybe you'll see me on the telly. That would be something.

Chalky just came over. He's got the wreath we're going to lay. He said, "Come on Elf, you first, you're the smallest."

Story of my life, really.

Three Finger Exercises

Andrea Gilbey

The Doll Maker

The woman in the upper window didn't notice the police car straight away. There were no flashing lights or sirens, no drama, and living on the main road through town, she was used to traffic buzzing past and had learned to zone it out.

It was only the flailing arm of the young woman who lived in the house opposite that attracted her attention. The girl was gesticulating wildly, her long red hair flying around in the light from her porch lamp as she tossed her head, pointing at the window where the woman stood observing calmly.

The two officers, a man and a woman, listened with their full attention on the girl, and the female officer wrote hurriedly in her notebook.

The woman in the upper window settled back in her chair to watch what unfolded, twirling between her fingers the long thick needle she had been using.

The neighbour finished her statement with an emphatic nod and a nervous glance at the house opposite and scuttled back into the safety of her own hallway, slamming her front door hard.

The female officer unlocked the patrol car, slid sideways onto the seat and spoke briefly into the radio on her shoulder. Reporting in. Locking the car again, the pair strolled casually across the road and disappeared from the watching woman's view, but she recognised the click of her own front gate and frowned. It must be some missing cat or dog that the girl was hysterical about.

Three Finger Exercises

Taking her time, resisting the urgency of the knock, the woman paced calmly down the stairs and opened the door.

"Yes, officers? Can I help you?"

She followed the female officer's staring eyes to the needle in her hand.

"Oh, I'm sorry, I was working upstairs."

The male officer cleared his throat.

"Good evening, madam, I'm sorry to bother you, but one of your neighbours has made some, er . . . unusual allegations. I'm sure it's all a misunderstanding, but she said she saw something very disturbing just now."

He glanced uneasily at the female officer who took up the tale.

"Um, yes, apparently you were seen at the upstairs window. . . ." She hesitated.

"Go on, I was seen . . . doing what?"

The nervous shared glance again. The younger woman licked dry lips.

"You were seen," she pulled out her notebook and read from it, using it to avoid eye contact, "stabbing a long needle through the head of a baby." She gulped.

"A dead baby," her partner chimed in, with gruesome relish. "It wasn't moving."

The woman looked at them, expressionless. She held the needle up and pivoted it slightly from side to side, the pair's eyes following the sharp point like kittens watching a feathery toy.

"A needle like this, you mean?"

The kittens nodded as one.

"And the hysterical girl thinks I'm some kind of . . . what? Murderer? Witch? Voodoo queen? You'd better come upstairs and see." She moved away towards the stairs, then turned back to look at her visitors, her face half in shadow, her glance steady, lip slightly curled in amusement. "If you can stand it, of course. Shut the door behind you."

Andrea Gilbey

The three trooped up the stairs in silence, the officers following the woman along a dimly lit landing to a bedroom at the front of the house. The room was dark, apart from a pool of light from a lamp on a desk in the window.

The woman ushered the female officer into the room, but the man stayed cautiously behind her, blocking the doorway. "In case I bolt," she thought, smiling grimly.

She flicked on the light and heard a gasp from the pair that quickly turned into a relieved laugh. The room was full of dolls. Rag dolls, each about two feet tall, each dressed in a different outfit, sitting, lying, standing propped, on just about every surface.

On the desk in the window was a sewing machine, and lying beside it, a half-finished doll, with no hair, no clothes and only one eye.

"This is what I was doing."

The woman crossed the room, picked up the doll, and showed the officers a small glass eye with a metal loop on the back. She deftly passed a piece of strong thread through the metal loop, doubled it, slid the two ends through the eye of the long needle, and stabbed the needle through the head of the doll. Seeing a curtain twitch across the road she held the doll up to the window and twisted it about to give her neighbour a good view, accompanied by the fake smile and posturing of a magician's assistant.

Hearing the young woman behind her snigger, she swiftly fastened the eye in place and threw the doll down on the desk, perching against the edge with her arms folded.

"Happy? No baby murdering happening here."

The male officer laughed, shaking his head, and prepared to leave, but his partner was in no hurry, prowling about the room, examining the dolls.

"These are so cleverly done; the detail is amazing! Do you sell them?"

"No," the woman replied, "it's just a hobby. They're caricature dolls, based on real people. Local people."

"Oh yes!" the younger woman exclaimed, picking up a male doll dressed in a grey suit, with slicked back dark yarn hair and small round glasses perched on its snub nose.

"This is that councillor, what's his name? The one who wants to close the community hall and stop all the funding for youth services."

"Didn't he have some kind of accident recently?" her partner asked, idly examining another doll dressed as a doctor.

"Yes, fell off a ladder cleaning his gutter, or something. He's in a coma in hospital with a broken back, poor thing."

The other officer was playing with the stuffed stethoscope around the doctor doll's neck.

"This one looks like that doctor who had that malpractice suit brought against her after that kid died. She got off, didn't she?"

"Yes, but didn't her practice burn down soon after? I thought I heard she killed herself, but I could be mistaken."

The doll maker was smoothing down the flared trousers of a male doll with a Bay City Rollers hair style and a fair isle pullover and looked up, only half listening.

"Oh, did she? That's a shame," she replied absently.

"This is my old geography teacher from school." She plonked the doll back down. "He was a terror, always shouting and giving detentions."

The police officers looked at each other.

"Is he . . . you know, ok? Still alive, I mean?" the girl asked.

"Yes, as far as I know. He retired to Spain, I believe. After his wife left him, that is. I believe there was some kind of falling out with his family; no-one ever hears from him now."

The pair laughed. "Oh, well, that's all right, then. It

just seemed a bit odd that two of these characters had bad things happen to them," the girl said in an apologetic tone.

The older woman smiled, but the smile didn't quite reach her eyes.

"The bad things that happen to some people are what they deserve."

The younger woman's smile froze at the harsh tone and she felt her lips dry and stick to her teeth. She ran her tongue around her mouth swiftly.

"Right. Come on then, Dave, we're finished here We'd best get back to the station. Sorry to have bothered you, madam. You're clearly a very talented artist."

"No trouble at all." The doll maker smiled, pulling the bedroom door closed behind her as they filed out onto the landing. "I'm glad to have put your minds at rest, and sorry you were troubled with this nonsense. Maybe that silly girl opposite will learn to mind her own business now."

***

The doll maker opened a drawer and pulled out a skein of red-brown yarn, holding it up to the light and tossing it about.

"I think this will do nicely, my pretty ones, but we'll finish her tomorrow; it's getting late."

She laid the yarn down beside the unfinished doll, straightened a couple of the collection who had slumped drunkenly, and walked to the door. Twenty-odd stuffed heads turned slowly and twenty-odd pairs of glass eyes followed her across the room and watched as she raised her hand to the light switch.

Something made her snap around and scan the room, her own eyes gleaming beadily in the light from the street lamp outside the window.

Twenty-odd calico faces stared blankly back, expressionless in the darkness.

Three Finger Exercises

Andrea Gilbey

Candlestick Lane

The sun was going down behind the boundary treeline, gilding the rippling buttercup meadow just the way it still did in my dreams. I turned to face downhill and scanned, shading my eyes against the low mellow light and trying to remember. It was uphill on the way out and downhill coming back, I knew that, but nothing looked familiar in a definite sense.

I followed the trampled path through the long whippy grass, tiny moths fleeing before my feet, the summer scent of mingled hot dry straw and freshly crushed green stems rising from the ground as I walked.

Usually a revisited childhood haunt looks smaller, not bigger. Maybe the place had been opened up? Or maybe we never explored this far? In which case, I wasn't going to find what I was looking for here, but still I strode on, uphill, waiting for a flash of memory.

At the top of the hill, the path dived into cool tangled woodland, rustling with the movements of small animals and echoing the startled clapping of pigeon wings, applauding their own skill in navigating between the branches. We had never come this far back then.

Later, yes, but with other people, and entering through the woodland gate from the road, never coming near the open spaces. I hadn't wanted to see them again when they were no longer mine.

Back down the hill, the fields spread behind me, the

surrounding houses hidden by the tree-lined hedges, as though the end of the parkland was the end of everything known, and beyond it the world spilled out into nothingness. Through a gap in the trees, the distant blue-grey skyline of London shimmered, like a far off fairy-tale city. So much of that skyline was new since I last came here. Was it really forty years?

I ducked into the woodland, following the path through mossy dampness, the cool green air slashed now and then by a bright sunbeam, a spotlight for the dancing midges. Memories of cook-outs stirred phantom woodsmoke scents, or maybe it was just a garden bonfire from the farms beyond the wood.

Laughter and singing, burnt fingers and mouths, charred sausages, scuffling out the fire, then running, running through the trees. . . .

The swish of car tyres on the lane at the back of the woods brought back a less welcome memory. The gap in the trees, a headlong rush out to the road, a dull thud and silence. The girl's white, still face . . . what was her name? She recovered, but we never went back to the woods for our cook-outs again.

But that came after.

My search hinged on happier memories of an earlier time, when going "over the field" was a Saturday afternoon treat longed for but never taken for granted, and sometimes, not every week, not every visit, there was the clamber over the stile to the special place.

Candlestick Lane.

Even the name was magical, but was it real? Had I made it up as the only way to preserve the wonder of those golden afternoons?

I circled round the perimeter of the wood and emerged into a sunlit mown meadow that hummed with the lazy conversation of small insects. A wire fence separated it from the practicality of the home farm, where geese were gossiping and arguing. An elderly couple strolled across the unmown neighbouring field, unaware of my watching eyes, their small dog leaping for joy in the long grass, appearing and disappearing like a bird startled from its nest.

Down the hill, a dead and scorched tree scratched at the blue sky and a memory stirred. Standing on a chair in my parents' bedroom, watching a storm through the window, safe and cosy indoors, but enjoying the drama outside. A crack, a flash of light, and a growing orange glow, just out of sight beyond the trees. An anxious wait, then the sound of a fire engine pulling in to the main entrance of the park. All safe, but even one tree lost from "my" park was the loss of a friend. The first grief of childhood. More grief was to come in a year's time, as Dutch Elm disease took more of my silent friends. That was the year we moved — not far, but to a place with a new field to play in, new paths to explore, and I never wanted to go back as a visitor from the other side of town, especially to the barren place my imagination created after the Great Felling, as I called it in my mind; the culling of diseased trees.

The Blasted Oak was part of known territory, something recognised, so I must be close. Would it even be there? How many elms had marched down that narrow lane, their branches joining hand overhead, and were they now all gone? The path wound around the side of the copse and there. . . .

Candlestick Lane.

Dark, green-shaded, cool and inviting, with patches of light glinting from above and aside through gaps in the scrappy uneven hedge and the heavy canopy. I stopped, stood, gazed, reluctant to break the spell, absorbing the reality of a place I hadn't seen for forty years.

Three Finger Exercises

I crouched to the height of a five-year-old. Yes, this was it. The path seemed wider; the place looked more managed; infant trees had been planted against sturdy sticks in little rubber support stockings, ditches cleared, benches added, and the stile, that magical gateway from an ordinary field that was such a mountaineering challenge to a three, four, five-year-old, was gone — replaced by a wheelchair access ramp across the ditch.

But the trees were the same, ancient twisted oaks, entwined with sweet-scented yellow honeysuckle, the vibrant flowers of red campion and the umbrellas of cow parsley nestling among the roots, and wild dog roses, heedless in their rambling summer-fresh youth, clambering over the venerable trunks. The sights those trees had seen — wartime bunkers, ugly against the wide fields, ladies in low-waisted flowing dresses strolling among the trees and, earlier still, tight-laced Victorians, ruffed Elizabethans and proud medieval landowners. Some of these trees would have been tiny saplings when the first house, now long gone, was rising on the top of the hill. Maybe some of the oldest had sheltered Romans tramping along Ermine Street.

The soft voices of those long-gone inhabitants seemed to rustle in the leaves. How long had this lane, now just a short tree-lined stretch of path, been a thoroughfare? I sat on one of the metal benches and leaned back against the trunk of a tree, closing my eyes against the sunshine that scattered through the leaves, and soaking in the scents and sounds. A pheasant barked in the woods and a small aircraft passed over, its sputtering engine dragging me back from ancient days.

Footsteps. People invading my reunion with this place.

A small girl, about three years old, was running towards me, a clutch of torn grass in her hand, laughing so hard she could hardly run. Her little tartan canvas T-bar shoes slapped against the hard earth as she pattered along and her short blonde bobbed hair glinted in the sun. She kept turning to look behind her as she approached, and a man came into view, running and laughing, his slightly flared brown trousers flapping above his shoes. Hipster dad, I smiled to myself, turning slowly to look at him. Everything outside of the scene before me seemed to slow down as he ran after the child, and my head felt muzzy and dull, as though someone had turned down the sound. The birdsong stopped and the rustling of the leaves faded away. The noise of the plane quietened.

The child trotted past, glancing back just as her foot hit a tree root. She tripped, stumbled, staggered . . . I reached out to catch her arm but the sun-induced lethargy made me slow and somehow I missed, my hand grabbing at thin air. She recovered and ran on, but her father had caught up, even though he was deliberately slowing his steps to let her feel as though she was winning. He caught her under the arms and swung her off the ground, and she squealed with delight as she pelted him with her handful of grass, most of which went down his collar.

He lowered her gently to the ground and dug the grass out of his shirt, shaking all over like a dog and laughing, although I knew it was playing havoc with his hay fever.

Knew?

Neither of them paid any attention to me on my bench, although they were only feet away.

"Now it's your turn to catch me. . . ." He trotted on ahead, still running at less than half pace, but some vague fear stabbed at me. I knew what was going to happen, what thoughts would go through her . . . my . . . mind and I rose to call out.

"No! Don't! She'll think you're leaving her behind. . . ." But I couldn't speak. It was as though a curtain hung between me and the two of them.

Three Finger Exercises

The child chased after him, but her laughter was turning to sobs as she ran as hard as she could but without any reduction of the space between them.

"Daddy! Daddy! Wait for me, don't run away, don't leave me behind. . . ."

The tears blinded me as I finally understood what I was seeing. But how? How could I be here both now and then? And he . . . why couldn't he see me "now"? Had I changed that much in the seventeen years since he ran on ahead and left me behind forever?

The figure ahead slowed, turned, crouched and held out his arms as the little one tumbled into them. He hugged her and soothed her, smoothing her hair and kissing the top of her head.

"Your old dad will never leave you behind, I promise, I was just playing, come here."

He sat on the bench of the stile and perched her on his knee, wiping her face with a big soft handkerchief and snuggling her in the crook of his arm until the sobs subsided.

"All right now?"

She nodded, sniffing and wiping her nose on the back of her hand.

"Come on, then, let's go home, it's nearly tea time."

They climbed the stile and their voices faded away across the field.

**

I sat motionless, shaken, tears pouring down my face as the sounds and scents of the summer day gradually returned. Was it a dream? I felt heavy and lethargic, as though all I wanted to do was lie down and sleep.

The small dog I had seen earlier gambolled past, sniffing at my feet, and his people came into view, laughing and talking. I snatched a tissue from my pocket and mopped my eyes as they approached.

"Are you ok?" The woman stopped, looked concerned. They were real, and now so was I.

"Yes, fine thanks, it's just hay fever," I lied, smiling at her. "My dad had it, too."

She nodded sympathetically, whistled to the dog and walked away.

**

I will go back to Candlestick Lane, now I know.

Not every week, not every visit, but I will go back. Maybe they will, too, protected from the future in their own little world where he will never leave her, and maybe I will feel their love again and see them once more.

Three Finger Exercises

Appendix – Notes on the Stories

The Fool on The Hill

This story came about after a visit to the Henry Moore gardens at Perry Green, Essex.

The huge bronze Reclining Figure sculpture set on a hill at the back of the gardens is one of the most impressive sculptures in the country and sits on man-made rise that looks to me like an Anglo-Saxon burial mound. It only took that thought and a friend jokingly describing the figure as "the fool on the hill" for this saga-style tale to start forming in my mind.

Sylvie and the Puh

A prequel story to my novel Bottletops For Battleships, this is an expansion of a story that my mother told me, of a misunderstanding between her and her own mother, which always amused me as a child and stuck in my memory. I don't clearly remember learning my alphabet, but I do remember the sudden "click" of understanding when marks on a piece of paper suddenly became letters and words.

The Ship's Carpenter

Inspired by an intensely moving visit to the Mary Rose Museum in Portsmouth, this story explores the idea that small children's minds are so flexible that they are possibly aware of other dimensions in time and space that exist alongside our own, and can sense the presence of people long gone. In other words, a ghost story.

Three Finger Exercises

Harvest Homecoming

This story was inspired by a photograph of American friends at a harvest homecoming back in the seventies, when they were teenagers and first dating. She is wearing a nineteenth-century prairie-style gown and sunbonnet and he is in modern dress, complete with zipped bomber jacker and shiny, pointed-toe shoes. The tale explores the idea of time travel as the main character experiences a time slip and meets his own ancestor, unwittingly becoming part of her history.

Sid and the Unicorn

My god-daughter, who was ten at the time this story was written, loves unicorns, and asked me to make her a unicorn toy based on the one from the film Despicable Me.

The unicorn was duly made and delivered, and shortly afterwards I was sent a photograph by my god-daughter's mother of the family dog, Sid, a Jack Russell, snuggling on the sofa with the unicorn toy.

I started wondering what the dog had made of the toy when it arrived, whether he understood that it was just a toy, or whether he thought it was somehow a rival for his young mistress' attentions.

A Plague on Both Your Houses

This was written from a writing prompt challenge on my good friend Marian Allen's blog; simply — "write a story about a rat."

Having kept fancy rats as pets, I knew this was a challenge I would enjoy, but I wanted to hide from the reader the fact that the subject of the story was a rat until the very end of the story, so I kept character description to a minimum and tried to make the reader believe that it was a tale about a homeless man.

110

Andrea Gilbey

Turbine or Not Turbine

A discussion (read disagreement) on a motorway journey with my boss lead to this sci-fi tale. As we passed a field of wind turbines I remarked on how elegant and awe-inspiring I considered them to be, to which my boss replied that he hated them. That pretty much ended the discussion, but it set me thinking. What if wind turbines had lives and personalities, and what if you *were* a wind turbine but didn't like being one?! I also enjoyed the challenge of writing a story in which the characters' communication could not be described using "he said" and "she said".

Just Desserts

This evolved from another of Marian Allen's writing prompts — "write about strangers sharing a meal".

The aim was to create a group of diverse and unconnected characters and bring them together under the watchful eye of a narrator who is part of the story, but slightly outside the main plot.

The Peace Bringer's Crossing

This is the first of two stories in this collection that have appeared in the Southern Indiana Writers Group's 2016 anthology XX: SIW GOES PLATINUM.

It is based on a painting by my good friend and fellow SIW member Joy Kirchgessner, of gondolas supported by hot air balloons flying towards the sun over a choppy sea. The story told itself to me as soon as I saw the painting, a print of which I am very proud to own.

Double Digging

The second story previously published in the Southern Indiana Writers' XX: SIW GOES PLATINUM, this one was written especially for the anthology. Having not long been elected a long-distance member of the group, I wanted to explore the idea of a group of people of various ages and differing characters united by a common interest and banding together to defeat a disruptive influence amongst them.

The Legend of Zen Koi

This short snippet of a tale is based on the gaming app Zen Koi, in which the player collects, breeds and hatches koi carp, then leads them around a pond catching prey until, on completion of all the required levels, the koi becomes a dragon.

The style is based on a children's TV programme form my childhood in which every episode contained a broken object which was magically restored by a group of toys and ornaments who came to life. Each object had a story, which was narrated by the title character, Bagpuss, in a dreamy, mythical style.

The Short Straw

This wartime story was inspired by the memory of meeting a former rear gunner at the local war memorial on Remembrance Day and listening to him relating stories about his experiences during the second World War.

I wanted the main character to tell his own story in the most immediate way possible, rather than have him look back and describe a memory, so I decided to use a diary format for the wartime action, then have him find the diary many years later and add a modern-day entry as an elderly man.

The Doll Maker

My first venture into horror, this story came about after an evening of sewing. Making a rag doll in my sewing room, I suddenly realised that I had left the blinds open after dark, and was highlighted in the window, with the light behind me, stabbing a long needle through a little calico body to finish the doll.

Andrea Gilbey

Laughing to myself at the thought of what passers-by would think was happening soon turned into rushing to the computer to put the story down.

Candlestick Lane

This is a very personal fantasy/ghost tale based on a true memory of sunny Saturday afternoons with my father in a place that seemed special and magical to a small child.

We moved to another part of town when I was five and, although I could have gone back at any time, I never wanted to until recently, in case I had imagined it, or the place was somehow spoiled.

It is still there, and still magical.

Three Finger Exercises

About the Author

Andrea Gilbey lives in leafy Hertfordshire with her two cats. She works full time in the fashion industry and enjoys drawing, painting, graphic art and photography to relax and unwind.

Andrea has published five illustrated children's books for pre-schoolers and upwards, and with Southern Indiana Writers colleague Ginny Fleming, worked on the *Written in Our Hearts Cookbook* in aid of the Davy Jones Equine Memorial Foundation.

Andrea's illustrations are inspired by friends, family and the world about her. She has written a non-fiction social history book, a children's novel, and is currently working on a sequel to her first novel, *Bottletops for Battleships*, which is set in wartime England.

www.ingramcontent.com/pod-product-compliance
Lightning Source LLC
Chambersburg PA
CBHW070602180626
46817CB00005B/1960